THE

BRONZE

DAGGER

Volume One: Ancient Elements

MARIE SONTAG

Mechanicsburg, Pennsylvania   USA

Published by Sunbury Press, Inc.
50 West Main Street, Suite A
Mechanicsburg, Pennsylvania 17055

www.sunburypress.com

NOTE: This is a work of fiction. Names, characters, places and incidents are the product of the author's imagination or are used fictitiously, and any resemblance to actual persons, living or dead, business establishments, events or locales is entirely coincidental.

For information about special discounts for bulk purchases, please contact Sunbury Press Orders Dept. at (855) 338-8359 or orders@sunburypress.com.

To request one of our authors for speaking engagements or book signings, please contact Sunbury Press Publicity Dept. at publicity@sunburypress.com.

ISBN: 978-1-62006-349-1 (Trade Paperback)
ISBN: 978-1-62006-350-7 (Mobipocket)
ISBN: 978-1-62006-351-4 (ePub)

SECOND SUNBURY PRESS EDITION: August 2014

Product of the United States of America
0 1 1 2 3 5 8 13 21 34 55

Set in Bookman Old Style
Designed by Lawrence Knorr
Cover by Daniel Sontag
Artwork by Raphael Lacoste
Dagger image by Kult of Athena www.KultOfAthena.com
Edited by Jennifer Melendrez

Continue the Enlightenment!

Dr. Sontag captures the Ancient Mesopotamia culture in a captivating tale of a young boy's survival. Armed with his lucky dagger, Sam sets out on an adventure where he encounters numerous challenges and foibles leading him to a lesson in forgiveness. A great read!
Dr. Donna Lewis, Educator: Assistant Superintendent

A terrific book for kids who like adventure, and for parents who'd love their kids to learn a bit about history. Well-written, a lively main character who struggles with his failures and searches for hope. Here is a hero who is flawed but resourceful, and who can lead readers on an adventure involving bad guys, jewels, new friends, and making choices. A real winner!
Karen Llewellyn., home-schooling mom

The book pulls you into history through well-written narrative. By the end of the tale you come away with not only an interest in the characters and storyline, but more knowledge about the time of the Babylonians.
Rick Crawford, former principal and author of Stink Bomb, and Ricky Robinson Braveheart

More information and teacher resources available at
www.thebronzedagger.com

If a son strikes his father,
they shall cut off his fingers.

From Hammurabi's Code

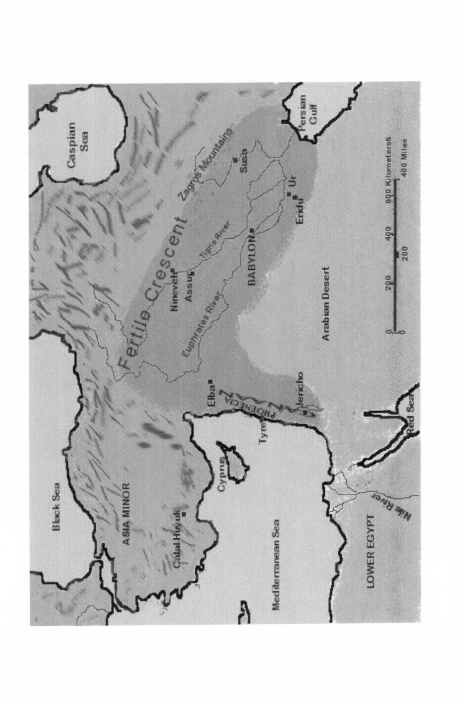

Chapter 1

"You! What are you doing behind our Bakery Shop? Shoo. Leave at once!" A bushy-haired boy, who looked about Samsuluna's age, took a threatening step toward Sam.

Twelve-year-old Samsuluna tried to stand but couldn't find his walking stick. Scrambling to his knees, he bumped into a large clay jar next to him. The jar tottered but refused to fall. "Please," Sam almost whispered as he eyed a bag of bread slung over the boy's shoulder. "Could you spare a small piece of bread?" Sam tried to remember the last time he had eaten. It had taken him all night to walk from the nearby Zagros foothills to the city of Susa. He hadn't eaten anything since yesterday afternoon.

"Ack! A beggar, eh? By the gods!" The boy wagged a finger at Sam. "You had better leave before my parents see you. They might have you arrested!"

In the dim light of the early morning, Sam tried to peer more closely into the boy's large brown eyes. "I'm not a beggar," Sam said. He found his stick, stood up and limped closer to the lad. "A cheetah attacked my sheep last night,

1

and I came to the city to find my uncle. Surely, you could spare a small morsel of bread."

The tightness in the bakery boy's face slackened. The boy removed the bread bag from his shoulder and started to withdraw a loaf when they heard muffled chirps behind the tall pottery jar on Sam's left.

"Gilgamesh, is that you?" the bushy-haired boy called out. The boys peered around the jar. There, on its side, lay a small brown and white bird.

Sam bent down to take a closer look. "I think its wing is broken."

"Gilgamesh, what happened to you?" The bakery boy crouched down and stroked the small bird's beak.

"When one of my sheep fell into a hole and broke her leg, I was able to fix it," Sam offered. "If we take Gilgamesh inside, I might be able to help."

The bakery boy nodded at Sam and then gently scooped up the injured bird, leading Sam through a side door of the Bakery Shop.

"My parents don't approve of pets," the bakery boy said. He carefully laid the bird on a low wooden table. "I found Gilgamesh near the marshes several weeks ago. A fox was raiding his nest when I came along and scared the animal away. Gilgamesh couldn't fly, so I brought him home and took care of him. By the way, I'm Enlil."

Sam pulled out a bronze knife from within his tunic. Enlil took a step back.

"Don't worry," Sam said. "I'm just going to put some medicine on Gilgamesh's wing." Sam withdrew a brownish-green nut from his leather pouch, cut a hole in it, and spread a green substance from it onto the bird's wing. He then limped outside and dug around in the weeds. He returned a minute later with an insect that he gently placed into Gilgamesh's beak.

"That might make him feel a little better," Sam said when he finished. "Enlil, I'm glad to meet you and Gilgamesh. My name is Samsuluna. You can call me Sam."

"Thanks for taking care of Gilgamesh," Enlil replied. The bakery boy removed a round loaf from his cotton sack and motioned for Sam to sit down on a nearby mat. Enlil tore off a large chunk and offered it to Sam as the boys sat across from each other at a low wooden table.

"So, Sam," Enlil started, "you were attacked by a cheetah last night?"

Sam finished chewing the bread in his mouth and then answered. "Yes. My sheep scattered, and I walked all night to reach the city. Since my parents are dead, I must now find my uncle." Sam avoided Enlil's eyes, finished off his bread, and then glanced around the tiny room.

"This used to be my older brother's bedroom," Enlil explained. "He got married last year and moved to Babylon."

Sam felt his chin begin to tremble. He stared down at his now empty hands. "Do you miss your brother?" Sam finally asked.

"Yes, I miss him terribly," Enlil admitted. "I come into his room whenever I feel lonely, and think about all the good times we had together. My parents never come in here. They say it will bring bad luck if they do, and then something bad might happen to Lurs. That's my brother, Lurs. He serves in one of King Hammurabi's top battalions in Babylon. Now that Lurs is gone, I have twice the chores I used to have." Enlil's eyes suddenly widened. "May the gods have mercy! I'm late for my deliveries! Sam, stay here and rest if you'd like. My parents won't know you're here if you're quiet. I have to deliver these loaves to the Grog Shop. And thanks for taking care of Gilgamesh." Enlil moved toward the door. "I'll return after my errands and then we can talk some more."

Sam brushed the remaining breadcrumbs closer to Gilgamesh. He then stretched out on a sleeping mat, but it was hard to sleep after the night he had, watching his older brother wrestle the cheetah that attacked them. Like letters carved into clay tablets, the scene now remained etched in his mind. Yasmah left Sam alone to watch the sheep. That night the brothers planned to run away from their landlord and search for their uncle. Yasmah went back to the landlord's house to find the bronze daggers the landlord took from them. The daggers were a parting gift to Sam and Yasmah before their uncle moved to Tyre.

Sam heard a rustling in the bushes, so he threw a rock in hopes of scaring whatever it was away. Then, when a cheetah snarled, he froze. The small cheetah suddenly leapt out and landed on one of Sam's favorite lambs. Without thinking, Sam beat back the cheetah with his staff. The cheetah turned to face Sam. It snarled once more, bared its teeth, and then pounced on him.

"Sam!" he heard someone shout. Yasmah had returned! His brother dove into the cheetah with a dagger and then stepped back. The wounded cat now turned on Yasmah. In the flickering firelight, Sam only saw the back of the cheetah's head and Yasmah's occasional lunges with the knife. Locked in a macabre dance, they tumbled for a few moments. Then it ended. The cheetah lay dead, blood trickling from its neck. Sam hurried over to where Yasmah laid, blood oozing from a gash in his side. The blood-soaked stains on his tattered tunic showed where the cheetah had ripped into the flesh of Yasmah's chest and arms. His breathing came hard and fast.

Sam whipped off his cloak and pressed it against the gaping wound in Yasmah's side. Sam's eyes widened and locked onto Yasmah's.

"Sam," Yasmah gasped for air. "I don't think I have much time. Listen carefully."

"Yasmah, don't talk like that!" Sam's voice cracked. "I am good at fixing wounds." Tears mixed with dirt flowed down his cheeks.

Yasmah gripped Sam's arm. "Listen, little brother," he said through clenched teeth. "I went to Ninkas' house to steal back our daggers, but I could only find one." Yasmah held the red-stained dagger up for Sam to see. "May it bring you luck. Take it and find Uncle Zim. He is all you have now."

"No! Don't say that!" Sam grabbed Yasmah by the chin as he leaned over him. "We will go to Uncle Zim together. You'll be fine! I'll take care of you."

Yasmah shook his head. "Reach inside my tunic," he commanded.

Sam reached inside and pulled out a bag of jewels.

"I couldn't find the other dagger, but these jewels were nearby, so I took them instead. The jewels will buy you food and passage to Tyre. Fate has decreed it. Go now, leave me." Yasmah's eyes squeezed shut in pain.

"No, brother!" Sam sobbed.

Yasmah never moved or spoke again.

By the time Sam awoke, the Mesopotamian sun had risen to the middle of the early autumn sky. Its warm rays filled the room, filtered through the linen cloth covering the window. Sam rose and checked on Gilgamesh. The bird now hopped around the tabletop, pecking at the breadcrumbs.

Enlil emerged from behind a curtain on the other side of the room, balancing a cup of tea in each hand. "I thought I would let you sleep," he said. Enlil placed the cups on the low table and sat down on a mat. "You looked as if you needed to rest. Now that you're up, however, perhaps you'll join me in a cup of barley tea."

Sam sat down and gratefully sipped from his cup.

"So, where in Susa does your uncle live?" Enlil asked.

"I, I am not sure." Sam looked at Enlil with a blank stare and then wrapped his hands around his warm cup. Sam didn't know yet how much of his story he wanted to reveal. Even with Enlil's kindness, Sam wasn't sure if he could be trusted.

"What does your uncle do for a living?" Enlil cocked his head to one side.

"He's a bronzeworker." Sam hesitated. "Actually, he doesn't exactly live here in Susa."

Enlil's dark brown eyebrows pinched together. "And your parents? You said they're both dead?"

Sam ignored Enlil's question about his parents. "The truth is, my uncle actually lives in Tyre."

Enlil shook his head. "I'm confused. I thought you said that after a cheetah attacked your sheep last night, you came to the city to find your uncle. If your parents are dead and your uncle lives in Tyre, whose sheep were you watching?"

Sam didn't want to tell Enlil about his wicked landlord, so he continued to talk about his uncle. "I didn't really say my uncle lives here in Susa. What I meant was, I walked all night from the foothills of the Zagros Mountains so that I could *start* my search for my uncle here in Susa." Sam took a quick sip of tea. "I had hoped to find a caravan here in Susa that could get me to Tyre."

Enlil's eyes narrowed. He looked at Sam a little more suspiciously. "And how did you plan to pay for passage to Tyre? That's more than a month's journey west."

Sam stared at his tea for a moment, swirling the liquid around with the cup between his hands. He had lost so much already. Slowly, he raised his head and looked into Enlil's doe-like eyes. "Can I trust you, Enlil?"

Enlil straightened up and leaned closer. "Yes," he replied.

"To tell you the truth," Sam spoke so softly that Enlil leaned over even more closely. "To tell you the truth," Sam began again, "the sheep belonged to our landlord. My father pledged my brother and me to him for a year of service to pay off our family's debts. My mother died while we were away and the landlord didn't even let us go home for her funeral. My older brother died last night trying to save me from the cheetah, so I ran away." Sam broke off,

8

gulped the rest of his tea and then placed his empty cup between them.

Enlil stared at Sam, waiting to hear more.

Sam slowly inhaled and then continued. "Before my brother died, he gave me these." Sam reached inside his tunic, withdrew a pouch from around his neck, and then emptied its contents onto the table. The facets of an emerald, diamond and ruby glinted in the sun in front of them.

Enlil let out a low whistle. "I should say, any *one* of those jewels could pay your way to Tyre and back again, several times!"

"Do you know of any caravans leaving for Tyre?" Sam asked. Carefully, he put the jewels back into his pouch.

"The gods must be with you!" Enlil exclaimed. "When I delivered the bread to the Grog Shop this morning, I heard that Negrel, a caravan driver, leaves tomorrow for Phoenicia. He spends every evening in the pub. You could meet him tonight and make your arrangements."

Sam nodded. "Yes, perhaps the gods *are* with me." He fingered the bronze dagger hidden under his cloak, and recalled Yasmah's words. *May it bring you luck.*

Chapter 2

Since Enlil's parents didn't approve of strays, whether birds or boys, Enlil advised Sam to wait out the day in his older brother's former bedroom. Enlil went out to make his afternoon deliveries and promised to return before sundown. After an hour, however, Sam grew restless. He fed Gilgamesh some bugs and placed a small dish of water on the table. He then tucked his dagger and jewels securely within the folds of his tunic and snuck out into the streets of Susa.

Rays of the late afternoon sun fingered their way through the narrow streets and cast long shadows behind women hurrying home with market produce. A silversmith's stall caught Sam's attention, and he stopped to admire the craftsman's work. Near the silversmith stood a man dressed in a white linen tunic fastened at the waist by a red sash. Sam had never seen such a well-dressed man before.

Sam watched the man in the white tunic give the silversmith a handful of coins. "By the gods, Igigi," said the rich looking man, "you must be the finest silversmith in all of Mesopotamia."

"Many thanks, Zama," the silversmith said and then smiled and bowed as he received his payment. "What is going on in Babylon these days?"

"Ahh, have you not heard?" Zama asked. "The Great Hammurabi has erected a black, eight-foot high stone pillar displaying all of his laws. This will force all judges throughout the land to uniformly apply the king's laws and decrees. No longer will judges be able to administer justice based on favoritism or bias."

Igigi gasped. "Never has such a thing been done!"

"So true, Igigi," Zama replied. "Hammurabi believes in justice, and does not want any of his subjects to be ignorant of his laws. Now, if only all of his subjects could read!" Zama laughed heartily.

Igigi leaned closer to Zama and asked, "So what are some of the king's new laws?"

Sam moved behind a large clay statue and continued to listen.

"Let me see," said Zama. He twirled the bottom hairs of his long gray beard and thought for a moment. "The king has laws about women, slaves, the rich and the poor, they cover just about everyone!" Sam watched Zama pick up a silver statue of the god, Marduk, which stood on the table between the two men. "For example," Zama continued, "if one of your customers took this silver statue without paying for it, you could have the thief's hand cut off, or even demand his death."

Sam nervously touched his chest where the stolen jewels lay tucked inside his tunic.

Zama continued. "However, the new laws also state that you cannot be convicted of theft unless the stolen property is found in your possession." Zama smiled and then added, "Yes, I dare say, our Great King Hammurabi wants to dispense justice equally to all." Zama bowed his head slightly. "May Shamash lengthen his reign, and may King Hammurabi reign in righteousness over his subjects!"

Sam left the stall before the two men noticed him. He continued to explore the streets of Susa. The smell of cooked onions, fish, and barley cakes floated out of nearby homes and into the streets. It reminded Sam of the family meals he used to have at home. Those memories already seemed distant.

Sam neared a corner and was about to turn when he overheard several men's voices. He stopped in his tracks.

"I treated them like sons," a scratchy voice cried out. "And that was how they repaid me, by stealing my jewels and running away! The older one got himself killed by a cheetah. You can be sure their father will pay, every last shekel, he will."

"But, remember, Ninkas," a thin voice replied. "Those jewels weren't yours to begin with!"

"Still, if I ever get my hands on the little urchin who stole them—"

Sam didn't wait to hear more. He quickly turned and hobbled back to the Bakery Shop. In his hurry, he ran into a young girl exiting the loomery. The two collided, knocking both of them to the ground.

"I'm so sorry," Sam blurted out. "I didn't see you." He struggled to stand and then offered his hand to the young girl who still lay sprawled out on the ground. He noticed that her beautiful yellow dress was now soiled with dirt. "Are you all right?" he asked.

The girl sat up, cradling her elbow with her hand. She winced as she looked up at Sam. "I'm afraid I scraped my arm rather badly," she said. A few drops of blood trickled out between the girl's fingers.

"It's all my fault. I'm so sorry," Sam apologized again. "Here." He gently helped the girl to her feet. When she stood, he saw they were about the same height and probably the same age. Her braided black hair had been neatly pinned to her head, but now it threatened to break free from its restraints. Sam awkwardly tried to brush the dirt off her gown. "If you come with me to the Bakery Shop," Sam offered, "I have an ointment that might help your arm feel better."

The girl hesitated, but then agreed, seeing the that Bakery Shop was only a few feet away.

Sam led the girl into the shop's side door. He dampened a clean cloth and cleansed her wound. He then took out the gall nut he had used for Gilgamesh's ointment and put some of its green sap on the girl's cut. At first she pulled away, but then she let Sam spread it over the entire scrape.

"It feels cool," she admitted. She smiled. "My name is Amata-Sukkal. I don't think I've seen you around here before. What's your name?"

"Samsuluna," he replied. "I'm only in Susa for a few days." He handed her the gall nut. "Here, take this with you. Put some of its sap on your cut every day for the next few days."

"Thank you." Amata said. "I hope to see you again before you leave." She lowered her head, smiled, and then slipped out the side door.

Sam sat down to catch his breath. Was it meeting Amata that made his chest feel tight, or was it because he had almost come face-to-face with his former landlord, Ninkas? Maybe both.

At sunset, Enlil brought Sam a barley cake and a small piece of cooked fish. Sam told Enlil about meeting Amata. He did not, however, tell him about Ninkas.

"Amata is the daughter of Balashi, one of Susa's finest *asus*." Enlil explained. "And she's rather pretty, isn't she?" Enlil added.

Sam felt his face grow hot. "I, I hadn't noticed," he stuttered. "I was too busy putting ointment on her cut. What's an *asu*, anyway?" he quickly asked.

"An *asu* is a healer," Enlil replied. "As an *asu*, Balashi's fame has grown much in the last few months, ever since he brought the governor's son back from near death."

Sam pulled a fishbone out of his mouth and swallowed his last bite of fish. "So tell me Enlil," Sam asked, "how can I meet the caravan driver tonight? Did you leave word for him that I'm coming?"

Enlil nodded. "Yes. The Grog Shop owner will tell Negrel to expect you. But give Negrel time to have a few drinks before you approach him," Enlil warned. "That'll put him in a better mood. And try to talk to him when he's alone. The men he hangs out with are nothing but trouble."

Sam thought about how his father acted whenever he had too much to drink. It never put his father in a better mood. Suddenly, Sam felt like a weight dropped into his stomach. He balled up his fists and dug his fingernails into his palms. Drunk or sober, Sam resolved to face the caravan driver. He just had to find his uncle.

Chapter 3

At the pub, Sam was pointed towards a large man with a scraggly beard sitting in the back corner. Negrel looked as if he hadn't bathed in months. He appeared about average height and weight, but the four husky men sitting at the table with him looked like men that no one would dare to cross. Sam nervously tightened the rope belt around his waist and then fingered the pouch of jewels hidden underneath his tunic. To bolster his confidence he patted his hip where he had secured his bronze dagger. The dagger! In his rush to get to the Grog Shop he had left it under the sleeping mat! His dinner rose up in his throat. Should he go back for the dagger before talking with Negrel? What if Negrel left before he got back? Sam hesitated for a moment and then approached Negrel's table.

"I hear you are Negrel, the caravan driver," Sam said, a little louder than he had intended.

Negrel turned and looked up at Sam. "So? What's it to you?" Negrel spat out. He then wiped his sleeve across his greasy mustache and beard.

Sam stood as tall as he could. "They say your caravan leaves tomorrow for Phoenicia. I want to go with you as far as Tyre," Sam said. Something about Negrel bothered Sam. Negrel's left eye never looked straight at him, but rather off to the side.

Negrel belched in Sam's face and then turned back around. The rude man drained his goblet and then growled, "I don't take children. I only take businessmen and merchandise." He waved a dismissive hand. "Go away. You annoy me."

Sam didn't budge. "Perhaps this will change your mind," he said. Sam withdrew the ruby from his pouch.

All heads at the table turned to eye Sam and the jewel. Negrel slowly reached for the ruby. Sam pulled it away. "You'll take me then?"

Negrel grabbed Sam's hand and wrenched the ruby out of it. "Let me take a good look at that, boy," he snapped. Negrel let out a slow whistle as he examined the gem. "Got any more like this one?"

"That one jewel should be enough to buy me passage from here to Tyre and back again," Sam remarked. He hoped he sounded assertive, but feared that his quivering voice betrayed his growing uneasiness.

The wooden bench scraped across the hardened dirt floor as Negrel rose to his feet. "Now, now, lad," Negrel soothed. He feigned a smile, clutching Sam's ruby more tightly in his oversized hand. "Nothing to get upset about. I was just asking." The caravan driver then reached out and grabbed Sam's shoulder with his other hand. "I prefer to make my business transactions outside. What say we step out into the night air and discuss my fees?"

Sam didn't have a chance to agree or refuse. Negrel's grip on his shoulder tightened as he escorted Sam toward the door. He saw Negrel glance back at the table and motion his head as if telling his men to follow. Negrel nudged Sam out the door and around to the back of the Grog Shop. A few seconds later, four large men also appeared.

"Now, lad," Negrel began, leaning his face so close that Sam had to turn away from the smell of his breath. "You see, my caravan is the *only* one headed toward Tyre for the next month. That's why my fees are so high. If you want to deal with me, it'll cost you more than this one jewel. What else have you got?"

Sam glanced around at the burly bearded men who now surrounded him. He wrapped his fingers even more tightly around his walking stick. His stomach twisted. Again his evening meal rose to his throat. Sam withdrew an emerald from the pouch around his neck and nervously held it out. "This, this is all I've got. You can have it too if you promise to take me with you in your caravan tomorrow."

Negrel let out a wicked laugh. He whipped the emerald out of Sam's hand. "Well, boys, do you think we should believe the little imp? He says this is all he has!"

Sam bit his lower lip and took a step back. How he wished he had brought his lucky dagger with him!

A man with beady black eyes moved forward to grab Sam's arm. Sam swung his walking stick into the man's shins and turned to run. He felt another man grab the back of his tunic. Sam quickly turned and jabbed the end of his stick into the other man's stomach. Sam then turned left to run around the side of the pub. In his hurry, he tripped over a rock and his stick flew out of his hand.

The beady-eyed man grabbed Sam by the back of his tunic and yanked him to his feet. "I think we should teach this brat a lesson," the man shouted, dragging Sam back to Negrel.

Negrel looked straight at Sam with his good eye. "First, search him," Negrel growled. "He says these two jewels are all he has. I don't believe him."

Sam tried to pull free from the beady-eyed man's hold, but it was no use. Another man grabbed Sam's other arm. A third untied the rope around Sam's waist and yanked it off. The fourth man searched Sam and found the remaining jewel, a diamond.

"I'll show you what I do to boys who lie to me!" Negrel shouted. The driver's face turned dark and ugly. "Believe me, you'll never lie to me again! Show him, lads." Negrel turned and walked away. The four large men closed in on Sam. One slapped him in the face. Another landed a blow to his stomach. Sam lost count of the punches. The full moon dimmed as Sam passed out.

Hours later, Sam dreamed that he had fallen into a lake. Feeling as though his lungs would burst, he tried to swim to the surface but his arms wouldn't move. Then he faintly heard someone call his name. His eyes flickered open and he saw Enlil standing above him. A light rain fell all around. He then realized he only dreamed he was drowning. In reality, it was early morning and he was lying outside the Grog Shop. He guessed he must have been there all night.

"Sam, Sam!" Enlil shook his shoulder. "What happened to you?"

Sam tried to get up, but pain shot through his right arm. His breath came in short, painful gasps. "My jewels!" Sam moaned as he slumped back down.

"You look terrible!" Enlil said. "Here, let me help you." Enlil bent down and carefully tried to lift Sam to his feet. Sam cried out in pain, and then began to shiver from the damp cold. Enlil dragged Sam out of the puddle. He then took off his own cloak and placed it over Sam. "Try to stay warm. I'll see if Balashi can come and help."

Sam wrapped himself in Enlil's cloak and fell back asleep. He had no idea how much time elapsed before he felt strong arms lift him up and carry him away.

The next time Sam opened his eyes he found himself in a warm bed. When he tried to brush some hair out of his face, he discovered his right arm in a splint, snugly wrapped in a white linen bandage. He attempted to take a deep breath but felt restrained. He looked down and saw his chest also wrapped in linen. "Wha, what happened? Where am I?" he groaned.

Amata's gentle face, framed by her long black hair, appeared above him. "Here, sip this," she said. Amata slowly raised Sam's head off the pillow and pressed a cup to his lips.

The warm liquid soothed his dry throat.

"You've slept for two days." Amata explained. "My father says you have a broken arm and broken ribs." She felt his forehead. "At least your fever's gone down."

Sam tried to sit up but the pain in his chest made him fall back onto the pillow. "My jewels." He groaned again.

"That's all you've said for the past two days," Amata said. "What are you talking about?"

Sam tried to draw in a breath, but only a puff entered his lungs. His head felt light. With the jewels gone, he had no way to reach Uncle Zim. What would he do now? Amata's face began to fade. He closed his eyes and fell back asleep.

The next day, Enlil came to visit. "I brought your bronze dagger," Enlil said. "You left it under the sleeping mat."

"Thank you," Sam said as he slipped it under his pillow. "If I had remembered to take it with me the night I met Negrel, maybe I would've had better luck fighting them off." Sam's eyes met Enlil's. He softly asked, "You haven't said anything to Amata or her father about Negrel, have you?"

Enlil pressed his lips together tightly and shook his head no. "I haven't told them much of anything about you. I figured you'd tell them when you were ready."

"Thanks," Sam said. He let out a sigh of relief. "You've been a true friend. Living in the Zagros Mountains, I didn't have any friends except my brother, and now he's gone."

"And so are your jewels," Enlil added. "You kept muttering about them when you had your fever. What are you going to do now?"

Sam's eyes blinked rapidly. "I, I really don't know. There's nothing for me back home in the Zagros Mountains. And now I have no way to get to my uncle in Tyre."

"Would the two of you care for some tea?" Amata said as she walked into the room carrying a tray. "Father says you should only stay a few more minutes, Enlil, so that Sam can get more rest."

"Actually, I should be going now," Enlil said. He stood up to leave. "I'm already late for my deliveries. I'll check in with you again tomorrow, Sam. I'm glad you're feeling better."

Enlil turned to Amata and bowed his head. "May the gods look kindly on your household. Many thanks to you and your father for helping my friend."

Three weeks later Sam sat on a cushion at a low, beautifully carved cedar table across from Balashi and his daughter. A servant in a white linen robe placed bowls of chicken soup in front of Balashi and Amata, and then one in front of Sam. As Balashi picked up his silver spoon, Sam ventured to speak.

"I am so grateful for your hospitality," Sam began. "I do not know how I can repay you." Sam stared across the table at the stern-looking face of the *asu* healer. He studied the dark brown beard peppered with strands of gray and wondered if the beard hid a softer face behind it.

"And I am grateful for the gall nut you gave my daughter," Balashi said. The *asu* sipped his soup and said no more.

Several minutes later, Amata broke the silence. "My arm is almost completely healed, Sam," she told him. "Father has never seen a wound heal so quickly. He has tried the gall nut on several of his patients with the same quick-healing results."

Balashi cleared his throat and glanced at Amata. She didn't speak again.

Sam glanced from Amata to Balashi. Both stared down into their bowls of chicken soup as they slowly finished their meal. Perhaps it was their custom to eat in silence. Sam did the same.

The following week, Balashi removed the linen bandages from Sam's chest and then invited him out into the garden for a walk.

"So, you tell me you are an orphan who left his shepherding occupation to come and find your uncle here in Susa," Balashi summarized as they walked down a dirt path between a row of leafless autumn trees. "Now that you are almost healed, how do you plan to find him? Do you know where he lives?"

Sam gulped and then explained, "Well, sir, he, he doesn't really live here in Susa. He actually lives in Tyre."

"Hmm, I see," Balashi commented. The *asu* stopped to observe his thyme and sage plants and then continued his stroll. "And how do you plan to get to Tyre? And how did you come to have a broken arm and ribs? You have never really explained this to me since we found you outside the Grog Shop."

Sam's face flushed. He hadn't told Amata or her father anything about the stolen jewels or his dagger, and he had sworn Enlil to secrecy. How much could he trust his new friends? Balashi had been so kind to take him in, and had asked Sam very few questions until now. Sam scrambled to think of an answer.

24

"I am not really sure how my accident happened, sir," Sam lied. "I had a fever when I reached the city of Susa, and went to the Grog Shop in hopes of finding food. The next thing I knew you found me and nourished me back to health, for which I am eternally grateful. As I've said, I don't know how I can ever repay your kindness."

"Well, you seem to have an interest, perhaps even a natural talent in the healing arts," Balashi admitted. "Perhaps you would consider becoming my apprentice? I could use some help in my work."

Balashi continued to walk down the path, hands clasped behind his back, but Sam froze in his tracks.

"You would consider making me your apprentice?" Sam asked incredulously.

Balashi stopped and turned to look at Sam. For the first time, Sam saw a gentle kindness behind the *asu's* dark brown eyes. "You have told me that you are an orphan and have no way to make the long journey to Tyre where your uncle lives," Balashi said. He turned his hands upwards and shrugged his shoulders. "As I said, I have been very busy, especially since I healed the governor's son. I, like you, search for natural ways to cure my patients. Since more of my patients seem to recover than those of other *asus*, more and more people seek my help. So, perhaps will you consider my offer?"

Sam couldn't believe his ears. For the past week he'd felt as though a dark cloud had continually hovered over his head. He had moped around the doctor's house, wondering what would become of him after he recovered from his injuries. Without the jewels, he had no way to get to Tyre to find his uncle. He couldn't go back to shepherding, and he certainly would never go back to his drunken father! And now the doctor had offered to make him an apprentice.

Chapter 4

The days dissolved into months. One cool spring morning, Sam and Amata collected balls of sap from the Nummlaria plant in Balashi's garden. Just as Balashi had instructed, they placed the congealed, pea-sized balls into sacks of barley flour for safekeeping,

"Amata, come over here and look at this strange thing I just found in my barley sack!" Sam said. He motioned for her to come over to his side of the garden.

"What is it?" Amata exclaimed as she rushed over. Looking down at his flour-filled hand, she frowned. "I don't see anything."

"Here." Sam pointed to the flour in the palm of his hand. "Look closer." Amata bent over to get a better look. Suddenly, Sam inhaled. "Ah, ah." Sam rubbed his nose and then let out a fake sneeze. Flour exploded everywhere. When Sam looked at Amata's floured face, he fell on the ground laughing.

Amata playfully kicked him in the side. "Very funny, Samsuluna!" She chastised him. "If you would stop fooling around and help me finish this work, perhaps Father will let us join Enlil down at the river before it gets too late. Remember? Enlil said he finished his raft. He told us to join him for a trip down the river if we got our work done early."

Sam had almost forgotten. So much had changed over the past few months. He, Amata and Enlil had become almost inseparable. In the mornings, Amata worked at her loom while Sam met with a tutor who taught him how to read. In the afternoons, Sam accompanied Balashi to visit patients. In the early evening before dark, Amata, Enlil and Sam often played board games or romped down by the river. Sam could not remember when he felt happier. For the first time in his life, the dark cloud that always loomed over his head seemed to have disappeared.

"Samsuluna!" Balashi shouted from the house. "I need those Nummlaria balls immediately. We need to visit the Priest of Nintu. His servant just came by and said the priest is complaining of severe stomach cramps."

Sam picked up his barley sack and tied the top into a knot. "If this doesn't take too long," Sam told Amata, "perhaps I can meet you and Enlil by the river when we're finished."

The visit took longer than expected. The Priest of Nintu insisted that Balashi also treat his wife and daughter who also complained of stomach cramps. After giving everyone the Nummlaria medicine, the priest asked Sam and Balashi to join him at the ziggurat for a thanksgiving offering to the mother goddess, Nintu. To refuse would offend the priest and his family, so Balashi agreed. By the time they left the ziggurat it was well past midday. Sam shifted the pouch containing Balashi's medicines to his other shoulder. *Amata and Enlil will surely have left without me by now*, Sam thought to himself as he kicked a rock on the way home.

"So, my young apprentice," Balashi interrupted Sam's thoughts, "If we use the Nummlaria sap to heal stomach cramps, do you recall what we use for coughs and chest pains?"

Sam thought for a moment. "I remember that when we visited Judge Mera last week you gave him droppings from the Teasel plant. I saw the judge yesterday and he said his coughing has stopped and that he is feeling much better."

Balashi smiled. "You learn quickly, Samsuluna."

Sam kicked another rock as they walked along the dirt path. Dust swirled up around them. "You do not believe in seeking the gods' help with your healings, do you sir?" Sam commented.

Balashi quietly walked beside Sam for a moment. His colorful robe flowed around him, twirling up even more curls of dust. Above them, a hooded crow cawed. Sam stopped and looked up just in time to see the crow flap its black wings to transport its large gray body from the top of one palm tree to the next. It reminded Sam of a story his tutor had taught him earlier that week.

Sam looked up at Balashi. "Do you believe the stories about the ancient gods?" Sam asked.

Balashi looked up at the crow. "Do you have a particular story in mind?"

Sam scratched his head. "Earlier this week, my tutor told me about the legendary Sumerian hero, Gilgamesh. He said Gilgamesh had an ancient relative named Ut-na-pish-tim. Supposedly, the gods once told Ut-na-pish-tim to build a large boat to save his family and relatives from a worldwide flood that the gods were about to send upon the earth. After the storm, Ut-na-pish-tim's boat rested on a mountain. Ut-na-pish-tim sent out a dove to see if the floodwaters had gone down. When the dove didn't find any food, it returned to the boat. The same thing happened when Ut-na-pish-tim sent out a swallow. After waiting for a period of time he finally sent out a crow. When the crow didn't return, Ut-na-pish-tim knew he and the others could safely leave the boat." Sam looked up at the crow again. "If that story's true, then maybe seeing this crow means I will have good luck today."

Balashi watched as the crow cawed again and then flew off. He gestured to Sam to continue walking. "Our people," Balashi began, "believe in luck and in the fate the gods deal out to us. I, however," Balashi paused for a second and then continued. "I suppose that I take after one of my ancient relatives, Abram. Abram could not go along with the idea of thousands of gods, such as a god who watches over your shovel, a goddess who watches over your cooking, a god of the water, one for the sky, the moon, war, the underworld, and so on. He believed in only one God. I've been told that Abram believed his God told him to take his family and move west to Canaan. Abram didn't believe in luck or fate. He believed in obeying his God and that his God was his friend. Perhaps I will go to Canaan someday and find out more for myself."

Balashi shrugged his shoulders. "Right now, however, I don't believe in any gods," the doctor admitted. "Mind you, I keep this to myself. I go along with our rituals to stay in favor with the rulers and my patients. Unlike most *asus*, however, I don't think luck, fate, or unseen gods have anything to do with healing. I suppose that is why I seek natural cures for my patients." Balashi patted the leather pouch that Sam carried for him and added, "And that is why we carry many more medicines with us than any of the other *asus*."

Sam pondered Balashi's words as they finished their journey home. Sam didn't agree with Balashi's views about luck and fate. Sam believed that he had been born into an unlucky family but that his bronze dagger had brought him good luck. Living with Amata and Balashi and becoming Balashi's apprentice, surely this good fate had been brought on by his lucky dagger. And now the crow would also bring good luck.

By the time Sam reached the river, Enlil and Amata were nowhere in sight. The late afternoon sun danced brightly off the water, inviting Sam for a swim. He dove into the cool water and swam out to his favorite rock.

Stretching out in the sun, he recalled some of the conversations he and his new friends had shared over the past month. Enlil had a secret desire to become a caravan driver so that he could see the world. Enlil knew, however, that his father planned for him to someday take over the bakery. Amata had shared some of the few memories she had of her mother. Her mother had died when she was six years old. Balashi's wife had contracted an illness that even the great *asu* couldn't heal. After suffering with a high fever for two weeks, she passed away. "Just before she died," Amata had said, her eyes brimming with tears, "Mother sang my favorite song." Now, lying here on the rock, Sam began to hum the melody that Amata had taught them. A few minutes later, Sam heard laughter drifting over the water. He looked up to see Enlil and Amata returning on Enlil's bamboo raft.

Sam stood up and shouted to them from the rock. "Hey! Over here!" Enlil and Amata continued their conversation and laughter without looking in his direction. Sam felt a chill, as if clouds suddenly covered the sun. But there were no clouds. "Why didn't they wait for me?" he wondered. Sam decided to play a practical joke. Without letting Enlil and Amata see him, he slipped into the water and swam out to the raft. He pushed up on a corner of it and managed to get the raft off balance enough to flip it over.

Amata screamed as she plunged into the cold water.

"By the gods," Enlil shouted as he splashed around trying to grab the raft.

Sam treaded water, threw his head back and laughed. "You didn't even see me coming, did you?" he teased.

Sam and Enlil righted the raft and then boosted Amata onto it.

"Sam, that was a mean thing to do," Amata fumed. She brushed strings of long wet black hair out of her eyes.

"Oh, come on," Sam prodded once they all boarded the raft. "If you don't want to get wet, don't get out onto the water. It was just in fun."

"Just in fun?" Enlil exclaimed. "Then so is this!" Enlil leaned over and pushed Sam back into the water. Surprised, Sam took in a gulp, went under, and then struggled to find his way back to the surface. All the while, he heard Amata and Enlil laughing above him. Sam thrashed about, trying to grab hold of the raft. Enlil paddled out of Sam's reach and headed for shore. Sam had no other choice but to swim in by himself.

"I'd better get home now," Enlil said after dragging his raft into a nearby cove and covering it with palm branches. "Maybe I'll see you tomorrow, Amata." Enlil left without saying goodbye to Sam.

"What's *his* problem?" Sam said as he and Amata began to walk home.

"He didn't appreciate your little joke," Amata replied. "And neither did I."

The two walked the rest of the way home in silence.

Sam didn't see much of Amata or Enlil over the next few weeks. Balashi had several patients to visit every day. Sam assisted him in sewing stitches, bandaging wounds and mixing and administering medicines. One day, after visiting the governor, Balashi took Sam to the Apothecary Shop. Balashi picked out several new herbs he wanted to try and handed the owner the small cylindrical clay seal that usually hung about his neck. "Please use my seal to show that I owe you for these herbs, Avara," Balashi said. He handed the owner his seal with an imprint of a bull. "I would like to take these herbs with me now. I will settle my account with you at the end of the month."

"Very good, Balashi," Avara said. The owner bowed, took Balashi's seal and pressed it into wet clay.

Balashi turned to Sam. "I am going to give you a copy of my seal to wear around your neck," Balashi said. "Then, if I ever send you on an errand to purchase goods for me, you may use my seal to pay for them." Balashi withdrew a leather cord from within his tunic. The cord held another cylindrical clay seal of a bull. Balashi placed this around Sam's neck.

Sam's chest felt tight. "I am not worthy of such a privilege," he said. Sam grasped the cord and began to lift it from around his neck. "I'm just a crippled orphan. I've done nothing to deserve such trust."

Balashi pressed the seal to Sam's chest, preventing Sam from removing it. "Trust is earned, Samsuluna, and you have earned my trust."

Sam felt a sudden urge to run away. He thought about all the half-truths he had told Amata and Balashi. He even thought about saying something to Balashi right there. Instead, he just looked down at his dusty sandals and said nothing. Sam limped out of the shop with Balashi at his side, doubting that he could ever live up to such a trust.

Later that evening, Sam and Balashi retired to the sitting room where they reviewed a scroll about new herbs that purportedly reduced fevers. Amata entered. In her hands she carried a three-squared board game decorated with a rosette. "Father," she asked, "would you join me for a round of the Royal Game of Ur? I might even let you win this time!"

Balashi absent-mindedly waved a dismissive hand without looking up. "Not now, Amata," he returned. "Sam and I are reviewing some new remedies."

"I understand," Amata quietly replied.

Sam looked up. Amata lowered her head and, narrowing her eyes, frowned at him as she stiffly strode out of the room.

Chapter 5

The next day, Sam found himself outside in the stifling heat to buy fish for Balashi, even though they just had a long, exhausting day of visiting the sick. Sam limped his way through the alleys and streets of Susa, struggling to breathe. As he passed the mud-brick homes where some of the more wealthy residents lived, he smelled lamb roasting somewhere over a fire. When given a choice, he'd much rather have lamb than fish, but he thanked the gods that he even had a home.

The winding streets now took Sam through a neighborhood where the homes stood more closely packed together. Suddenly he sensed a familiar smell that made his mouth water. The image of his mother suddenly appeared in his mind. Turtle soup. That was it. It had been his favorite. Someone here was making it with the same herbs and spices his mom had used. That time now seemed so long ago.

As Sam neared the marketplace, he thought about the past few weeks. He and Balashi had never been so busy. Was that why Sam hadn't talked with Amata much lately, or was it something else? Ever since the incident on the raft, they barely said anything to each other. Girls. How was he supposed to understand them? He never had a sister, and he never had any girls as friends when he lived in the Zagros foothills. If Sam and Yasmah ever had a problem, they worked it out by punching or wrestling with each other. He figured that wouldn't work with Amata. Before long, Sam found himself at the bazaar in front of the fish market stall. He picked out a few carp and catfish and then gave the fishmonger Balashi's seal. After pressing the seal into wet clay, the seller wrapped up the fish in date palm leaves and handed them to Sam.

Suddenly, off to his left, Sam spied Amata at a jewelry stall. He saw her gazing at a lapis lazuli necklace. He was close enough to see that the highly polished, intense blue stones contained gold-colored inclusions of pyrite that sparkled in the sun. He watched Amata sigh as she reluctantly handed the necklace back to the merchant. Certainly, Sam thought, such a necklace would cost a prohibitive sum, even for the daughter of an important *asu*. As Amata turned to leave, her eyes met Sam's. She turned back around, as if she hadn't noticed him.

"Are you walking back home now?" Sam asked, coming up beside her.

"I just have one more stop," she replied, without looking at Sam. She let her gaze fall back on the lapis lazuli necklace. "I have to pick up a tunic and a shawl at the loomery."

"If you'd like, I could go with you and help you carry the packages," Sam offered. "I just finished buying some more fish for tonight's dinner." Sam held up the date palm leaves.

Again, Amata did not look at Sam. "If you wish," she replied. Amata whirled around and walked toward the loomery.

The two walked together in silence.

When they arrived at the shop, the seamstress held up a white linen tunic for Amata's inspection.

"It's beautiful," Amata said as she slowly nodded her head and smiled.

"Let's make sure it's the right length," said the seamstress. She pressed the garment to Amata's shoulders. "Yes, that looks perfect. You just gather it here in a bunch on your left shoulder. You can clip it or make a tie loop to hold it in place." The seamstress gathered the material at the left shoulder to demonstrate before she continued. "And, as I'm sure you know, you wear it off your shoulder on the right. Fasten your favorite belt around your waist, add a few pieces of select jewelry, and you'll turn many heads!"

Amata blushed.

Sam pretended not to notice and focused his attention on other garments hanging in the shop. He admired the quality of the flaxen linens, remembering the coarse flaxen garments he had worn when he lived in the Zagros Mountains.

"What about the shawl?" Amata asked as she took the gown from the seamstress and laid it on a wooden table next to her.

"I think you will be pleased." The seamstress smiled. She went behind a curtain and then quickly returned with a blue linen shawl. She placed it around Amata's shoulders. The edges flowed down below her waist.

Amata touched the golden fringe that encompassed the shawl's hemline. "It's beautiful," she said softly, drawing the cloak more firmly around her shoulders and lightly brushing her hand over the softened linen.

Sam looked at Amata. "Yes, it is," he agreed. He knew he wasn't just talking about the shawl.

Once again Amata's cheeks brightened. She looked up at Sam with a slight smile.

"Now, what about slippers?" the seamstress asked. "I have some nice gold ones here that match your shawl's fringe." She pointed to a delicate set of footwear on another table. "Or perhaps you would prefer these blue ones?" She held up a blue-dyed pair of woolen slippers with leather bottoms. "Both pairs look about your size."

Amata tried on the blue woolen slippers. "Yes, these will do." She removed Balashi's cylindrical seal from around her neck to pay for the merchandise.

The seamstress wrapped the gown and shawl in a flaxen cloth and then did the same with the slippers.

"Here, I'll carry those for her," Sam offered.

Amata held back Sam's arm. "I'll take the gown and shawl package," she said. "Why don't you just carry the shoes? I don't want the garments to pick up any fish odor."

As they left the shop Sam asked, "What are these beautiful garments for? Do you have a special occasion coming up?"

"Father heard rumors that he might get a promotion," Amata replied. "If he does, it'll be announced at a special ceremony and we'll all be invited. He suggested that I buy myself a new gown for the event." Amata hesitated and then added, "Actually, I think he was just trying to cheer me up."

The two walked together in silence for a moment. Then, suddenly they both spoke at once.

"Sam."

"Amata."

Sam laughed. "You can go first, even though you're a girl," he teased.

"Sam," Amata started hesitantly, "I, I'm sorry that I haven't talked to you much lately. I've been feeling a little, oh, I don't know what I've been feeling. That's my problem." Amata grimaced and then walked along in silence again.

"I'm sorry about the raft," Sam apologized. "I didn't mean to hurt your feelings. I only meant it as a joke."

"I guess that's part of it," Amata continued. "I was enjoying some time with Enlil and I felt like you interrupted us." Amata bit her lower lip before she went on. "You see, lately, you and Father have spent so much time together that I guess I felt left out. I was trying to explain that to Enlil when you flipped over the raft."

Sam scratched his head. "I don't understand," he admitted.

"That's just it Sam," Amata said, shaking her head. "You don't understand." She wrinkled her nose and looked over at Sam. "You seem like you're always walking around with a cloud over your head. I feel like you're holding back, sharing part of your life with us and yet hiding some dark secret. It seems like you don't trust us, or anybody. You're like a bird with a broken wing. You traipse around the city with Father, healing the sick, but you can't seem to heal yourself."

Sam swallowed hard. No one ever spoke to him so honestly before. "And what does Enlil think?" he asked. "Does he feel the same way?"

"Enlil believes you trust him more than anyone," Amata admitted, "but he knows that you don't really fully trust him either. He wants to be your friend, but he doesn't know what more he can do."

Sam felt a burning in his chest that began to move up to his throat. "You're right," he managed. "I don't know what to say." He shrugged his shoulders, and they walked the rest of the way home without speaking.

Chapter 6

A few days later a Babylonian messenger arrived while they were eating dinner. A servant escorted the messenger into the dining room and Balashi silently read the clay tablet the palace messenger handed him.

"What is it, sir?" Sam asked.

"I have been offered a position in Babylon as a court physician," Balashi explained. "I heard rumors that I might receive such an invitation." The *asu* stroked his beard and looked across the table at Amata before he continued. "The Great Hammurabi has heard of my work here in Susa. He wants me to come to Babylon as soon as possible." Balashi looked up at the messenger. "Tell the Great Hammurabi that he can expect my reply by the end of the week." The messenger bowed and left.

"May I read the message, Father?" Amata asked.

Balashi slid the tablet across the table to Amata.

Sam felt his chest swell as he watched Amata read the message. Well-to-do fathers only trained their sons to read, not their daughters. Daughters were usually only trained to cook, weave, garden and care for children. However, as Sam had learned, Balashi was not one for traditions. As Amata read the cuneiform figures pressed into the clay

44

tablet, he noticed that her expression did not change. Sam couldn't tell if she felt happy or sad about the news.

"You mentioned that you might get a promotion," Amata said. She pressed her lips into a flat line, and then continued. "But I thought it would just be a more important position here in Susa. Would you really consider moving to Babylon?" Amata slid the tablet back to her father.

Balashi reached into a bowl in the middle of the table, withdrew a large fig, and took a bite before answering. "Amata, moving to Babylon could open many doors of opportunity for us."

"You mean it could be a good opportunity for you and Samsuluna," Amata said. She put her hands on the table and leaned toward her father who sat across from her. "I have many good friends in Susa, Father, and you have more than enough patients right here." Amata's pitch rose. "I don't want to leave our home. I have so many good memories of Mother here."

Balashi frowned, his forehead furrowed. "We must consider what's best for all of us." He paused and studied his daughter's reddened face before he continued. "I have something else on my mind that I want to discuss with both of you." He cleared his throat and leaned toward Sam. "Sam, you have done a wonderful job as my apprentice. How would you like to officially become part of our family?"

Sam's eyebrows arched. "You mean, adopt me?" he asked.

"That's right, my boy. Since your parents are dead, and you aren't really sure where your uncle is, I would like to officially adopt you as my son."

Sam felt lightheaded. Adopted by Balashi and a possible move to the capital city! By the gods, how could he be so lucky? He then thought about the half-truths he had told Amata and Balashi. Suddenly, he felt totally unworthy. He looked down at his crippled leg. Feeling nauseated, Sam searched Amata's face to gauge her reaction. Amata burst into tears and ran out of the room.

Amata's response confirmed Sam's sense of unworthiness. Sam struggled to stand and then bowed in front of Balashi. "By the gods, sir, it would be a great honor to have you adopt me," he said. "Taking me in as your apprentice, that was already more than I deserved. But to adopt me as your son?" Sam's words caught in his throat. "I am not worthy to be your son. You and Amata deserve better. I do not want to come between the two of you."

Balashi slowly stroked his beard before he replied. "I will speak with Amata. Perhaps this is too much, too soon." Balashi then stood and placed his hands on Sam's shoulders. "I have come to love you like a son, Sam. You have the potential to become a great *asu* some day. I want to help you develop that potential. A father gives his children love, not because he deems them worthy, but because they are his children. Trust is earned, but love must be freely given. You have earned my trust, and I would freely like to show you my love by making you part of our family. Think on it some more, and we will talk about it again at the end of the week."

Amata avoided Sam the rest of the week. He prodded her to talk, but she just turned away. Sam tried to put himself in her place. Since the age of six, Amata's family only included Amata and her father. How could she be asked to open up her family to a third person? Sam's stomach twisted. He, Enlil, and Amata were becoming such good friends. They were, in fact, the only real friends he'd ever known. Now he found it all unraveling.

That night, Sam couldn't sleep. What should he do? He didn't dare tell Balashi that his father was still alive. What if Balashi sent him back to the Zagros Mountains? How he longed to be part of a real family where he felt wanted and appreciated instead of hated and abused. Obviously, Amata didn't care for the idea of his adoption. Balashi and Amata had been too kind for him to come between them. What could he do? Last month Balashi began to give him an allowance for his work as an apprentice, but he didn't have enough yet to strike out on his own.

Sam doubted they would understand, but by the end of the week, he made up his mind. Without telling anyone, he would "borrow" some money from Balashi in order to buy passage to Tyre. Once he found his uncle and started earning his own money, he would repay the good doctor.

Sam waited until everyone went to sleep, and then he quietly crept downstairs to the cabinet where Balashi kept his coins. He carefully counted out 15 shekels and placed them in the leather pouch around his neck. He then patted the dagger under his tunic just to be sure he still had it. With one last look around the house, he disappeared into the night.

Chapter 7

By the time the sun rose to mid-morning, Sam reached the town of Tepe Guran. When he passed a bakery stall his stomach growled, begging for bread. Sam started to reach for the pouch under his tunic. Should he spend the money? He feared he would need all of it for passage to Tyre. Then he remembered Balashi's seal. He still wore it around his neck. He and Balashi had visited Tepe Guran before and Sam knew the merchants here accepted his seal. He hurried back to the bakery stall.

Sam waited until some soldiers placed their orders. He then stepped up to the baker. "Two loaves of bread please," he ordered. He took off his seal and handed it to the baker.

The short, heavy-set owner wrinkled his long pointed nose as he looked at the seal. "So Balashi wants this on his account, does he?" the baker said. "Just a minute, lad."

Sam looked over the other bakery goods on display as the owner finished up his business with the soldiers. Suddenly a dark shadow fell over Sam.

"Where did you get this seal, boy?" The taller soldier asked as he stepped up behind Sam. In his hand, the soldier fingered Balashi's seal.

"Please, sir," Sam said as he turned to face the soldier. "I, I am an apprentice of the great *asu*, Balashi. He gave me his seal to make purchases for him."

"Well, I think you should come with me until I can verify your story with the *asu*," the soldier replied, grabbing Sam's arm. Sam had no choice but to go with him.

The soldier searched Sam and confiscated the 15 shekels and his bronze dagger. He spent the rest of the day in a cold, damp cellar. By evening, a guard came and took Sam upstairs to a waiting area. A few minutes later another soldier entered, accompanied by Balashi. Sam felt so ashamed he couldn't even lift his head.

"Well, Samsuluna," Balashi said as he entered the room. "I wondered why you hadn't returned home yet with the bread I sent you to pick up."

Sam gave Balashi a puzzled look, as did the two soldiers on either side of him. The taller soldier spoke first. "You sent this boy all the way from Susa to Tepe Guran for a loaf of bread?"

"Ah, it is very special bread!" Balashi explained. "And I also gave him 15 shekels to purchase special medicines at the Apothecary Shop here in town." The *asu* looked at Sam with twinkling eyes. Balashi then turned to the soldiers and said, "I think you have wasted enough of our time. Would you please release the boy into my care now?"

It was too late to walk back to Susa that evening, so Balashi found an inn for the night. Sam finally broke the silence as they entered their room. "Why didn't you tell the soldiers the truth?" he asked.

"And what is the truth?" Balashi said as he washed his face in the ceramic water basin on the bamboo nightstand.

"I stole your money and seal so that I could go to Tyre and find my uncle," Sam confessed.

Balashi dried his face and hands before he responded. "Samsuluna, I care for you as if you were my own son. Everything I have is yours. If you do not want me to adopt you, if you would rather go to Tyre and find your uncle, just say so. I want what is best for you."

Sam felt his lower lip quiver. He'd never known such love and acceptance. Tears escaped from the corners of his eyes. "But I don't deserve your love and trust," he blurted out.

"Children don't have to deserve their parents' love," Balashi said. He walked over to Sam and brushed the dark bangs out of his eyes. "Parents love their children because they are their children. Trust, on the other hand," Balashi's added, "can be earned and lost. Taking off with my shekels and seal, I admit, has shaken my trust in you. If you choose to become part of our family, we will have to work on rebuilding that trust."

Sam began to sob. He wrapped his arms around Balashi and buried his face in the gentle man's robe. "But Amata is your true child, not me," Sam cried. "She doesn't want you to adopt me. Don't you need to do what's best for her?"

"Sometimes children do not always know what is best for them,' Balashi soothed. "Amata has already lost her mother, and she was afraid that, if I adopted you, she would also lose her father. However, she and I talked last night. She truly does care for you as a brother, Sam. After you left, she realized how much she wants you to be part of our family. It just took her a little longer to figure that out. Now wash and get ready for bed," Balashi instructed. He ruffled Sam's hair. "When we get back to Susa tomorrow we have a lot of packing to do!"

Amata and Balashi tried to describe Babylon to Sam, but nothing prepared him for the sight of the majestic structures he saw two weeks later as he crossed the moat and entered through the large city gates. When Sam passed a huge Babylonian ziggurat, his mouth dropped open and he stopped in his tracks.

"What is that?" Sam asked, pointing at the huge rectangular-stepped tower.

"The building is called *Et-em-en-an-ki*," Balashi explained. "It means the temple connecting the sky and earth. This magnificent temple is one of the great achievements of Hammurabi."

Sam stood transfixed as Balashi pointed to the structure and continued. "The temple is almost 298 feet high. It has seven levels, each smaller than the last. And, as you can see, an elegant staircase connects each floor." Sam continued to stare as Balashi went on. "There are 600 rooms, each dedicated to a different god. All of the rooms are richly decorated with precious stones. Each room also has many statues. Hammurabi brought together the best craftsmen in the land to fashion the statues out of gold or bronze. And some are carved out of wood from the cedars of Lebanon."

Sam gave out a low whistle, craning his neck to see the top. "Surely the gods must be pleased with such an enormous building!" he exclaimed. "No wonder the Great Hammurabi has been able to live in peace!"

Amata tugged on Sam's robe, encouraging him to continue down the road as she took over as tour guide. "Only a local maiden is allowed on the top floor of the temple," she explained to Sam. "And the top level has only one room. This room contains a bed and a solid gold table, and it's said that Marduk stays there each time he returns to Earth."

Sam looked up ahead and to his left, then pointed to a large palace. "Is that where the Great Hammurabi lives?"

"Yes," Balashi replied. "And our new house is not far from it."

They turned down an unpaved side street and passed a row of single-level mud brick houses. None had any windows facing the street. They then turned down another street and saw rows of two-story plastered and whitewashed mud brick dwellings. Balashi stopped in front of one of them. "This is our new home!" he announced.

Chapter 8

After their first month in Babylon, Sam began to feel at home. Amata continued her studies with a reading tutor in the mornings. In the afternoons she worked with female servants who taught her skills in weaving and cooking. They had their evenings free for reading or play. Sam enjoyed his early morning rounds with Balashi, making house calls on important capital officials who had various ailments. In the afternoon, he and Balashi usually saw patients in the palace.

Summer gave way to autumn. Late one evening he and Balashi were summoned to care for Hammurabi's son who complained of a stomachache. He had eaten an entire cake earlier that evening and only admitted it when Balashi insisted that the boy tell him everything he had eaten that day.

A week later, when the family had retired to the sitting room after a late dinner, they heard a knock at the door. A servant announced that two young soldiers had arrived and they were asking to see the great *asu*. Balashi told the servant to let them in.

The two men entered the sitting room, one leaning on the other. Sam noticed something familiar about the injured soldier, but he couldn't figure out what it was.

"Please sir," the injured man looked at Balashi. "I have come all the way from Susa to see you. I was injured in a skirmish with nomads from the Zagros Mountains. I stayed in Susa to heal, but my injury only worsened. The *asus* in Susa told me I should come to see you when I returned to Babylon."

Balashi rose from his wicker chair. "Follow me," he told the two men. "And, Samsuluna, come with me also," he added as he escorted the men into one of the servant's bedrooms.

"Lie down and let me examine you," Balashi directed the wounded man.

The injured soldier removed a pouch from around his waist and placed it on the bamboo table next to the bed. Then, after lying down, he lifted up his short, red tunic. "I was stabbed in the chest," the soldier explained, "and, as you can see, it began to heal. Before long, however, it grew red and irritated and opened up again. Now it feels hot to the touch."

"Samsuluna," Balashi instructed, "wash the wound and then put aloe on it while I prepare a tumeric compress."

"Yes, sir." Sam said. He quickly went to the medicine room, retrieved the aloe and returned to the soldier. "So you were in Susa for awhile?" Sam asked as he washed the wound and then applied the thick liquid aloe. "We just recently moved here from Susa."

The soldier nodded yes and then winced as he tried to sit up. "My battalion is stationed here in Babylon, but we were sent to help out a battalion in Susa," the soldier explained. "The Susa battalion had trouble rounding up some nomad bandits who were hiding in the foothills of the Zagros Mountains. We tracked them to a local tavern in one of their villages, but they put up a good fight as you can see from my wound. My parents live in Susa, so I stayed behind to recover while the rest of my battalion brought the prisoners back here to Babylon."

"Perhaps that's why you look familiar!" Sam shouted. "Do your parents own a Bakery Shop in Susa?"

"Yes, they do," The soldier said and then smiled. "My brother, Enlil, told me that if I saw you, I should be sure to say hello. You are young Sam, Enlil's friend, correct?"

"Yes!" Sam exclaimed. "Is Enlil still mad at me for dumping him over on his raft?"

"He told me about that." The soldier smiled again. "Enlil says he isn't mad anymore and that he misses you and Amata. He hopes you both come back to visit soon."

Balashi returned with the compress and interrupted their reverie. "This compress must be changed every few hours," Balashi instructed. "By the way, what is your name, young man?" he asked.

"He is Enlil's older brother!" Sam blurted out.

Balashi furrowed his brows and Sam lowered his eyes. "Sorry, sir," Sam apologized.

The injured man offered, "I am called Lurs, sir."

The other soldier who had been quietly standing in the corner cleared his voice. "Excuse me, Lurs." he interrupted. "Will you need me any longer?"

"I don't think so," Lurs replied. "Do we, doctor?"

"No," Balashi said, shaking his head. He then turned to the other soldier. "Thank you for bringing your friend. Tell your captain that Lurs will need to stay with us for a few days."

The other soldier nodded and then left.

"And how did you say this happened?" Balashi turned back to Lurs and secured the compress into place with linen wrappings.

"As I was telling young Sam here," Lurs began, "my battalion was sent out from Babylon to help the Susa battalion capture some raiding nomads living in the Zagros Mountains. The nomads raid sheep and cattle owned by the good people of Susa and some even break into shops. They always run back to the foothills to hide. One evening we discovered that they were holed up in a local pub in a Zagros mountain village. We surrounded the tavern and captured all of them, but they put up a good fight. The rest of my battalion brought the prisoners back here to Babylon while I stayed behind in Susa to heal. After a while the Susa *asus* realized there was nothing more they could do for me, so they sent me back home and advised me to seek you out."

"Balashi is the best *asu* in all of Babylon," Sam said, beaming.

Lurs shifted his weight on the bed, biting his lower lip against the pain. "Actually, I'm almost grateful for my wound," Lurs admitted. "Three weeks ago my wife gave birth to our first-born son here in Babylon. Now I have a good excuse to stay home for awhile while I recuperate." Lurs pointed to his pouch on the nearby table and instructed Sam, "Before I forget, hand me my pouch."

Sam obeyed.

Lurs opened the pouch and withdrew a small clay tablet. "Enlil wanted me to give you this," he said, handing the tablet to Sam.

Sam read it over and then excused himself to find Amata. "Amata!" he shouted, finding her in the sitting room. "Read this. It's from Enlil!"

Amata put down her sewing and read the tablet aloud. "Sam, I overheard a conversation while delivering bread to the Grog Shop. Negrel plans to go to Babylon soon to form a new caravan headed for Tyre. And Negrel still has your jewels!"

Amata handed the reddish-brown tablet back to Sam. "Is this the caravan driver you told me about?" she asked. "The one whose men beat you up and then left you for dead outside the tavern in Susa?"

"That's the one," Sam said. Over the last month Sam confided in Amata and told her about the jewels his brother stole from Ninkas. The only thing he hadn't told her was that his father was still alive.

The color drained from Amata's face. "Sam, you're not thinking of trying to get those jewels back, are you?"

Chapter 9

A few weeks later, Sam and Balashi were summoned to the barracks of the palace guards. Like Lurs, the Susa battalion's captain had come to Babylon to recuperate from an injury he had sustained in the battle against the Zagros Mountain nomads. He hadn't returned to Susa yet because his broken arm hadn't completely healed.

"It's a good thing you called for me," Balashi said after examining the captain's arm. "Whoever tended your broken arm in Susa didn't splint it correctly. If you ever hope to wield a sword or dagger again, we need to re-break the arm and set it correctly."

The captain fingered the hilt of the dagger hanging from his side. Sam saw a wave of anger flood his eyes. His nostrils flared as he took in a deep breath. "The *asu* in Susa who tended my arm will certainly hear from me!"

Sam eyed the captain's dagger more closely. He noticed three round indentations in the hilt. He asked, "Captain, why are there indentations on your dagger?"

The captain's eyes softened. "My great-grandfather gave me this dagger shortly before he died," he explained. "He was a mighty warrior in battle. The hilt used to contain three jewels, but they were stolen from me about five years ago when I became battalion captain in Susa. My men threw me a welcoming party when I first arrived. I knew many of them from my previous assignment in Ur. We had a little too much to drink that night, but somehow I managed to make it up to my room at the inn. I neglected to secure my door, however, and when I awoke the next morning, my dagger was gone. I found it later, outside in the rubbish heap, but the jewels were missing." The captain paused and looked down at his misshapen arm. "By the gods, I swear, Susa has held nothing but bad luck for me ever since!"

Balashi turned to Sam. "I'm afraid my job here will take longer than I expected," he said. "We were supposed to see Lurs next at his home. Will you go and tell Lurs that I'll come by later this afternoon?"

Sam bowed. "Yes sir," he enthused. Lurs had stayed with Balashi for a few days, but was now finishing his recuperation at home with occasional visits from the *asu*. Because of Lurs' new baby, Balashi occasionally sent Sam or Amata to check up on the family and to lend them a hand. Sam enjoyed visiting, playing with the baby, and hearing Lurs' stories about military life.

"Sam, come in!" Lurs' wife greeted him. "We have a surprise for you today. Look who just arrived from Susa!"

Behind Lurs' wife stood a bushy-haired boy.

"Enlil!" Sam shouted as he ran over and grasped his friend's shoulders. "It's so good to see you! What are you doing here?"

The boys sat down on mats near the eating table where Lurs' wife had placed a bowl of pears.

"When my parents heard about Lurs' injury, they sent me to help," Enlil explained. "Mother would have come herself, but my father can't run the Bakery Shop without her!"

"Neta," Enlil looked up, "since the baby is sleeping now, would you mind if Sam and I took a walk?"

"Not at all, Enlil," Neta replied. "Just be back in time for dinner."

"You know me," Enlil said, giving her one of his broad, toothy grins. "I'm never late for a meal!"

Sam took Enlil to see Hammurabi's eight-foot high stone monument in the palace courtyard. "So how is life in the big city?" Enlil asked Sam.

"It's so exciting!" Sam exclaimed. "Balashi has taught me much about the healing arts. I've also learned to read and have even soaked up some knowledge about politics!"

Sam pointed to the black stone pillar that loomed in front of them. "For example, this tablet contains Hammurabi's laws. I've been told that no other ruler has written down his laws for all to see, such as Hammurabi has done. Other rulers often change their decrees whenever they feel like it because there's no publically written record of them. But in Babylon, Hammurabi, his governors, and his judges all have to provide the same penalties for the same crimes. They can't favor one person over another, for example, just because a criminal might be a good friend of the judge. See?"

Enlil nodded yes.

Sam pointed to one of the columns on the stele. "Read what it says here."

Enlil craned his neck upward and read aloud. "'I am the salvation-bearing shepherd whose staff is straight. My staff's good shadow spreads over my city so that the strong might not injure the weak, and to protect the widows and orphans.'"

Enlil looked over at Sam. "So, King Hammurabi is not just a money-hungry ruler living up in his palace. This makes it sound like he really cares about the people."

Sam looked down at his crippled leg. "I always hated people in power. Especially my father," he added in a low voice. "To me, people with power always represented pain and injustice." Then, thinking fondly of Balashi, he added, "I had no idea it could be any different."

Sam and Enlil continued to scan the tall black obelisk.

"Look at this law," Enlil said. "It talks about adoption." Sam drew closer as Enlil read out loud. "'If a man adopts a child as a son and rears him, this grown son cannot be demanded back again.'

"And here's another." Enlil's voice grew more excited. "'If an artisan has undertaken to rear a child and teaches him his craft, he cannot be demanded back.'

"Well, nothing for you to worry about," Enlil said. "Since both your parents are dead, there's no one to demand you back."

"Right," Sam replied. He wet his lips and then drew them into a straight line.

Enlil continued to read out loud. "If anyone steals the minor son of another, he shall be put to death."

Sam's eyes widened. He pushed Enlil aside and moved in for a closer look. He read the law again to himself. *If anyone steals the minor son of another, he shall be put to death.* Sam pondered its meaning. Could this law apply to him? If court officials found out that his father was still alive, could Balashi be put to death for adopting him without permission?

Just then, the boys heard angry shouts in the next courtyard. They walked through a stone archway and out into an open plaza. A few yards away a group of about twenty prisoners stood chained together in front of a raised platform. On the platform a tall bearded man sat under a canopy in a high-backed stone chair. The bearded man wore a gold-colored robe and a gold cone-shaped hat. Guards in red tunics surrounded the prisoners, nudging them with spear-tips. An angry mob stood behind the guards and shouted obscenities. Some people in the mob threw rotten tomatoes and cabbage at the prisoners.

The bearded man in the stone chair glared down at the prisoners beneath him and shouted, "You men of the Zagros Mountains have been charged with theft, and causing bodily harm to soldiers of our great king, Hammurabi."

Sam wanted to get a better look at the prisoners, so he slowly squeezed his way through the sweaty-smelling mob. After he managed to wind his way to the front, Sam couldn't believe his eyes. About eight feet away from him stood his father. Instinctively, he patted his robe to make sure he still had his lucky dagger strapped to his side. He did.

Chapter 10

Sam quickly slipped back through the crowd to find Enlil.

"Sam, what's the matter?" Enlil said when he saw Sam's whitened face. "You look like you've seen a ghost!"

"You might say that," Sam said, licking his dry lips.

The judge in the high-backed chair reviewed a tablet in front of him and then said, "I understand there are others here from Susa who have also brought charges against these men."

"Yes, I have other charges," a scratchy voice called out from the crowd. Sam saw the scrawny figure of Ninkas, their family's creditor and landlord, wriggle out from the center of the mob and move toward the front.

"One of these men owed me the labor of his two sons for one year," Ninkas cried out as he shook his fist in the air. "After only two months, one son got himself killed while watching my flocks, and the other ran away. I demand retribution!"

Sam wondered why Ninkas didn't say anything about the stolen jewels.

"Have the man that you accuse brought before me," the judge told Ninkas.

Ninkas pointed out Sam's father. A guard unchained him from his fellow-prisoner and then pushed him into a kneeling position in front of the judge.

"What is your name, prisoner?" the judge asked Sam's father.

"Dagon, sir," Sam's father replied without looking up.

"And what do you say to these charges?" The judge asked.

Sam's father hung his head. "The charges are true," Dagon muttered. "I owe Ninkas more money than I can repay."

The judge leaned over and looked down at Sam's father. "If you cannot repay your debt, then you will serve a year in prison here in Babylon," the judge declared. "Any sheep, cattle or other goods that you have will be turned over to your creditor to help pay your debt. This case is now dismissed."

Sam felt hot and sweaty. He didn't want to hear any more. "Enlil, let's go down to the river. I need to think."

Sam took Enlil to one of his favorite spots along the Euphrates River near a stand of willow trees. The river flowed through the capital of Babylon and was busy at every point except for a section near these trees. Under their shade lay two large boulders. Sam and Enlil sat with their backs against the boulders and skipped stones across the surface of the Euphrates.

Sam finally broke the silence. "Enlil, I'm in a lot of trouble," he confessed. "I feel like I've made such a mess of things and I don't know what to do."

"I'm listening," Enlil said.

Sam skipped a few more stones before he spoke again. "You know the man we saw today? The one who owed the creditor money?"

"Yeah," Enlil said.

"He's my father."

Enlil looked at Sam wide-eyed and exclaimed, "I thought your parents were both dead!"

Sam put his head in his hands. "I lied," he admitted. "And now my father will spend the next year in jail because I ran away from our landlord. And, if that's not bad enough, what if my father found out that I've been adopted without his consent?"

Enlil just gaped at Sam and slowly shook his head.

Sam moaned and then continued. "According to what we read today, if my father found out that Balashi adopted me without his consent, he could cause the *asu* a lot of trouble! And then there are the jewels that Negrel stole from me that were originally stolen from Ninkas, our creditor, which were stolen from him by my brother!"

"Wa, wait!" Enlil interrupted. He held up his hand and leaned toward Sam to get further clarification. "Let me get this straight. You're not really an orphan and you've been adopted without your father's consent. You ran away from your creditor and now your father must go to prison."

Sam nodded.

Enlil took a breath and then continued. "And, if that wasn't enough, the jewels that were stolen from you were actually stolen by your brother from someone else?"

"That about sums it up!" Sam said as he threw a stone into the river.

Enlil whistled. "You're right. You are in a lot of trouble!"

The next afternoon Sam and Enlil met again by the willow trees. Sam noticed Enlil's left eyebrow rise when Enlil saw that Sam brought Amata with him.

Sam explained, "Enlil, both you and Amata have been such good friends to me. I thought that perhaps the three of us could figure a way out of this mess together."

Amata sat down with the boys next to the boulders. "Well, running away is not an option," she began. "You've already tried that Sam, and we will not allow it to happen again."

Sam smiled. The assurance of Amata and Enlil's friendship helped to calm his uneasy stomach.

"Let's tackle the adoption problem first," Enlil said. "What's the worst thing that could happen if you asked your father's permission to let Balashi legally adopt you?"

Sam pulled at the clumps of grass around his feet. "My father could say no," he slowly began. "And I'd have to go back to the Zagros Mountains and work for Ninkas for another eight months. After that, I'd have to go back and live with my father." Sam shuddered.

Amata pouted. "That doesn't seem fair."

"No, but it is *just*," Enlil said. "And if you continue to pretend that your father is dead, the truth will probably come out eventually, and that could make things bad for Balashi."

"Amata," Sam turned to his half-sister. "You know that I would never do anything to hurt you or Balashi. I must do what's right and just. I see that now."

Amata turned her head away, stood up, and then ran down to the river. Sam started to go after her but Enlil grabbed his arm.

"Let her alone for a bit," Enlil said. Sam nodded and sat down again.

Enlil scratched his head and then asked Sam, "What about having to work another eight months for your landlord? That's really your *father's* debt, isn't it?"

"Yes," Sam agreed, "but by law my father can legally hire me out to pay off his debts."

"But," Enlil interjected, "what if you came into some money and were able to pay off your father's debt?"

Sam thought for a second before he answered. "Then I suppose I wouldn't have to work for Ninkas. But how could I —"

"Remember the jewels?" Enlil asked. His eyebrows shot up and a slight grin warmed his face.

Sam opened his mouth, but nothing came out. Finally he asked, "You mean the jewels that Negrel stole from me? What good are they to me now? Besides, they were never mine in the first place."

Enlil smiled his toothy grin and then remarked, "I'm not quite sure, but I have a hunch that they might come in handy."

Suddenly the boys heard a splash and then a scream from Amata. They ran down to the river.

Sam bit his tongue to keep from laughing. The river's edge was muddy and he could see by the indentations in the mud that Amata had taken three steps before she slipped and fell into the shallow water. She now flailed her arms in an effort to regain her balance. The more she tried to stand up, the more she slipped, and the more she bathed herself in mud.

Enlil put his hand over his mouth to suppress his laughter as he saw Amata's face and arms plastered in wet goo.

"Well don't just stand there!" Amata shouted. "Someone get me out of here!"

Chapter 11

The time for secrecy had ended. Sam confided in Balashi concerning his father, the landlord, Negrel and the jewels. Sam felt a great weight lift from his shoulders. No matter what the outcome, Sam knew he could face whatever happened as long has he had the love and support of Balashi, Amata and Enlil.

Balashi arranged for a meeting between Sam and his father. Gray clouds gathered overhead as Balashi and Sam entered the dank prison compound. Guards guided them through cool stone corridors until they reached the section that housed Sam's father. The stench of human sweat and waste assaulted Sam's senses but did not dislodge his resolve to confront his father. His father's small cell housed eight other prisoners. All of the prisoners sat on the dirt floor with one arm shackled to the rock wall. Sam went in to face his father alone while Balashi waited outside the cell.

"Hello, Father," Sam began in a low voice.

Sam's father lifted his head, looked up at Sam, growled, and then looked down again. "How dare you even call me Father," Dagon said. "You desert your dead brother, run away from your obligations, get me thrown in prison, and then dare to call me Father!"

Sam grit his teeth. He figured his father would blame him for everything. He tried to steel himself against the accusations. "Father," he began, "I'm sorry you were put in prison because I ran away from Ninkas. I will try to make that right. However, I have come to ask your permission on a very important matter." Sam paused and then took a step back before he continued. "Since I left Ninkas, I've come under the care of an *asu* here in Babylon. He thought you were dead, so he took me in as an apprentice. Now that he knows you're alive, he'd like your permission to legally adopt me."

Dagon slowly lifted his head and looked up at Sam through the long, greasy black hair that covered his eyes. A cruel smile crept across his face. "I suppose you wish I *were* dead," Dagon spat out, "dear son of mine, *only* son of mine! Then you would be free of all you owe me!" Dagon yanked his shackled arm away from the wall as if trying to free himself. The chain rattled as he pulled his arm taut, but then he let his arm fall limp. In the dim light, Sam could see his father's eyes squint in anger as he twisted his face to look up fully into Sam's eyes. His father whined. "And what is to become of *me* if I let this doctor adopt you? Who will care for me in my old age?" Dagon turned his head away.

Sam shifted his sandaled feet. This was not going well.

Dagon turned to look up at Sam again and added, "That is, unless this *asu* is a very *rich asu*! Perhaps he would be willing to pay me a healthy sum for the privilege of adopting you!" Dagon's mouth twisted. He lifted up his hand as if to strike Sam. Sam pulled back, but then realized his father's chains kept him out of reach.

Dagon laughed and continued his rant. "Perhaps the *asu* would pay enough to cover Ninkas' debt and then an additional sum to make my life a little more comfortable from now until I die. What do you think?" Dagon's mouth twisted again. "Does this doctor care for you *that* much?" Dagon snickered. "Huh. I doubt it! What good are you, a poor, crippled boy!"

Sam's lower lip trembled. Both anger and shame flooded his heart. He would never ask Balashi to pay his father for the "privilege" of adopting him. He would rather go to prison himself. Why was his father so hateful? Sam recalled Balashi's words when Sam had tried to run away. "Children do not have to deserve their parents' love." That would never be true for him.

That evening Balashi invited Lurs' family to join them for dinner. Lurs announced that he had some exciting news to share but insisted that it wait until they completed their meal. Amata, Enlil and Sam finished their dinner quickly, but then had to sit quietly until the adults finished eating.

"Ah, that was a magnificent meal, Balashi," Lurs complimented as he stretched out his arms. "Well, we better get home. The baby fell asleep quite some time ago." Lurs saw the look of horror on Sam's face and winked at Balashi.

"You can't leave without telling us the news, Lurs!" Sam almost shouted.

"Oh, yes, the news!" Lurs teased. He walked over to where he hung his uniform's overcoat and withdrew a clay tablet from within. He then returned to the table and handed the tablet to Balashi. Lurs explained, "My Susa captain is holding a banquet here in Babylon next week to honor new commissions. My captain has been promoted to head up three battalions here in Babylon, and I have been promoted to command the battalion stationed in Susa!"

"That's wonderful news," Amata exclaimed as she clapped her hands.

"Thank you. Yes, it is good news," Lurs agreed. "It will be wonderful to be near my family again, especially with the new baby." Lurs looked over at Balashi. "The tablet is your invitation, good Balashi. The captain has invited you and your family to his commissioning banquet out of gratitude for the healing work you did on his arm."

Sam stared straight ahead for a moment and then turned to Lurs. "When a new battalion leader is placed in a city, isn't there usually a change in city leadership?"

Lurs thought for a moment before he answered. "I suppose so. Usually the outgoing battalion leader appoints new city officials whom he knows will be loyal to the king and who will help make the transition smooth. Why do you ask, Sam?"

"Oh, I'm just reviewing what I've learned about politics to make sure I've learned my lessons correctly," Sam said. He looked at Amata and winked. Sam had a plan.

Chapter 12

The next day Sam and Enlil sat down with Lurs and unfolded to him Sam's story and his plan. After Sam explained about Negrel and Ninkas, Sam then related his plan for getting the jewels back. The first part of the plan involved inviting Negrel and Ninkas to the commissioning banquet. Sam thought it best if the invitations came from Lurs, and Lurs agreed.

As was his custom, Negrel usually hung out at the local tavern when he wasn't busy preparing for the next caravan drive. Sam and Enlil, with the help of Lurs' wife, baked several loaves of bread and took them to the Babylonian pub frequented by Negrel. Enlil told the tavern owner that his family sold bread to shops in Susa. He then suggested that his family might expand their business to Babylon, and asked if the owner would like to try out some free samples on his guests. The owner agreed and gave the boys two knives to slice the bread. Sam declined a knife and pulled out his bronze dagger instead. Sam promised himself that he'd never leave home again without his dagger. While the boys cut the bread, Sam pointed out Negrel to Lurs, who immediately took up a seat next to Negrel.

"I understand you are from Susa," Lurs began, after waving down a helper to bring him some ale.

"What of it?" Negrel growled.

"I've been appointed as the new commander of the battalion in Susa, and heard that you might be a good businessman to have in a leadership position."

At this Negrel sat up straight, drained his goblet, and then cleared his throat before speaking. "Well, I do know a lot of people in Susa and have quite a bit of influence on them, if that's what you mean."

"That's exactly what I mean." Lurs said as he clapped Negrel on the back. "The outgoing captain of Susa is throwing a banquet next week, and I would like to give you an official invitation." Lurs withdrew a small clay tablet from his tunic and handed it to Negrel. "Now, it is very important that you make a good impression on the former Susa captain at this banquet. You see, afterwards, he and I will discuss our leadership choices. He has the final say. Because of the things I've heard about you, Negrel, I really hope you can be one of those people that we discuss."

Negrel tugged on his beard and then cleared his throat again. "Do you have any suggestions of how I can make a good impression on the captain?" he asked. "I'm sure that having some kind of leadership position in Susa would go a long way toward helping my caravan business."

"I like the way you think, Negrel," Lurs said and then smiled. "There is one thing the captain has talked about a lot lately, but, well, they are hard to come by."

"What is it?" Negrel pressed. The caravan driver leaned forward and looked intently at Lurs with his one good eye. His other eye wandered off to the left.

"Well, you see, he has a fondness for jewels," Lurs said. "Especially emeralds, rubies, and diamonds. Actually, it's his wife who's just crazy about them. You see, she doesn't really want to leave Susa. She hates it here in Babylon. But the former Susa captain has just received a great promotion and must relocate here to the capital city. If he could find the right emerald, ruby or diamond as a gift for her, I'm sure he would be extremely grateful!"

A slow smile spread across Negrel's face. "I just might be able to get my hands on one of those jewels," he said. "Which do you think she'd prefer?"

"Well, you see, that's the dilemma," Lurs replied. "The captain's wife is so moody that she changes her mind from day to day. If I were you, and if I had all three of those jewels, I'd bring all of them to the banquet. I can easily find out her mood that evening, and let you know. Then, at the right time, you can present the perfect jewel to the captain. I'm sure that would earn you the attention and position you deserve!"

Sam and Enlil continued to pass out the bread as Lurs and Negrel talked. "Sam, I'm thirsty," Enlil said when they were almost finished with their distribution. "Let's ask the owner for some water."

The boys approached the owner where he stood behind a counter to serve ale, and asked for water. As the owner filled two tin cups, Sam noticed that Negrel paused in his conversation with Lurs. Negrel nervously looked around the room.

Sam leaned over and whispered into Enlil's ear. "I don't want Negrel to see me here. He might remember me from Susa and suspect something's up. I'm going to move to the back of the room until we're done."

Enlil nodded in agreement. Sam slipped his knife back into the folds of his robe and then moved to the back of the room. Enlil looked over at Lurs and Negrel. At that moment, Negrel looked up and noticed Enlil at the counter. Negrel cocked his head to the side, as if trying to remember where he might have seen Enlil before. Negrel then nudged one of the men sitting next to him and whispered. Enlil looked away and continued to sip his water.

"My guests seem to like your bread," the owner told Enlil. "If your prices are less than what I'm paying my current baker, I think we can make a deal."

At that moment, the man next to Negrel came over to the counter and asked the owner for another pitcher of ale. Enlil turned his head away and stared at a group of men on his left. When Enlil turned back, he noticed some green powder sprinkled on the counter. He nonchalantly drew circles in it with his finger while he finished his water and watched Negrel's table. He then set his cup down next to the powder and moved slowly toward the door. Sam crept out from the shadows and the two boys slipped outside. Lurs joined them a few minutes later.

"Whew, that was close," Enlil exclaimed as they began to walk home. "Did Negrel take the bait?" Enlil asked Lurs.

"I've got him hooked!" Lurs beamed.

"For a moment, I thought Negrel recognized me," Enlil said. "When he sent thon wee vu wha." Enlil stopped mid-sentence. His arms began to twitch. His legs wobbled. "I feel, can't the see volley."

"Enlil, what's wrong?" Sam shouted.

Lurs caught Enlil just before he fell to the ground.

Chapter 13

"What's wrong with Enlil?" Amata shrieked as Lurs carried Enlil's convulsing body into one of the servant's bedrooms.

"He was fine one moment," Sam explained, "and then he just started talking funny and twitching all over."

Balashi heard the commotion and rushed into the room. "Did Enlil have anything to eat or drink?" the *asu* asked as he leaned over Enlil's spasmodic frame.

"Just some water at the Grog Shop," Sam volunteered.

"Sam, bring me some mustard and black charcoal powder," Balashi ordered.

Sam hesitated, staring at Enlil in disbelief.

"Now!" Balashi barked.

Sam blinked then ran out of the room.

"And a pitcher of water," Balashi shouted after him.

Balashi examined Enlil's face, arms, hands, and legs. "I can smell honeydew melon, although it is faint," Balashi said just as Sam returned. "And there seems to be a green powder on his fingers."

Amata, trembling, held her hands to her face. "Father, what is it?" she asked. "Is he going to die?"

Lurs stood back in silence.

"I've got the mustard, charcoal powders and water," Sam offered.

"Quickly Sam," Balashi snapped. "Mix one part mustard powder to five parts water. And Lurs," Balashi shouted, "hand me that empty bowl and the towel from the table over there. Amata, lift up Enlil's head."

Everyone quickly obeyed. Balashi put the mustard mixture to Enlil's lips and made him drink.

A minute later Enlil leaned over, retched, and then vomited into the nearby bowl.

Next, Balashi added charcoal powder to a cup of water and made Enlil drain the cup again. Enlil continued to twitch and utter nonsensical words. Panic-stricken, Lurs, Amata and Sam stared at each other.

Sam felt beads of sweat trickle down his forehead. "It's all my fault!" Sam cried. "I never should have asked him to go with me." Sam grasped Enlil's twitching arm. "You've got to be okay Enlil. You've just got to."

"Samsuluna," Balashi soothed, laying his hand on top of Sam's. "We have done what we can. You must let the poison work itself out of his system."

"But he can't die, he just can't. It's all my fault," Sam repeated.

"Your panic will not make him heal any faster," Balashi said firmly. "I think you should go outside and let me tend to him. I will call you if anything changes."

Sam wiped his tears on the sleeve of his brown tunic, turned, and walked away.

An hour later Balashi found Sam out in front of their home staring up at the stars.

"We never should have gone to the Grog Shop. It was a stupid plan," Sam muttered. "Is Enlil going to die?"

Balashi stood quietly next to Sam for a moment before answering. "No. The worst is over," he said. "He is resting now. If we hadn't treated him right away, however." Balashi's voice trailed off.

"What was it?"

"I smelled honeydew melon and found traces of a green powder on his fingertips. You said he had a cup of water at the Grog Shop?"

"Yes sir."

"I suspect someone poisoned his water with green lotus powder, which is very poisonous. It causes a twitching of the limbs, blurred vision and slurred speech. It can be fatal if not treated immediately."

Sam sat down in the dirt, leaned his back against their mud-brick house, and poured out his thoughts. "I think Negrel recognized Enlil from Susa and had one of his men poison him." Sam picked up a few pebbles from the ground near his feet and then flung them into the dark night. "I don't belong here. I almost got my best friend killed by asking him to help me. And my real father. I hate him. He refuses to release me. I wish he were dead. He doesn't deserve to live. I should just go to Tyre to find Uncle Zim."

Balashi sat down next to Sam. He also picked up a few pebbles. He shifted the stones from one hand to the other before he spoke. "Finding your Uncle Zim will not solve your biggest problem, Samsuluna."

"And what is my biggest problem?" Sam asked with a petulant shake of his head. "Is it finding a way to pay back Ninkas for the jewels I stole? Or is it that I lied to you about my father being dead and got you to adopt me illegally? Or is it that I seem to hurt everyone who gets close to me, everyone I love?" An ache exploded inside Sam's chest as he thought about his dead mother and brother. Tears spilled down Sam's face, but he didn't bother to wipe them away. Instead, he hid his face in the folds of his robed arm. Waves of uncontrollable sobs rose from deep within him.

Balashi let Sam cry for a minute. Then Balashi whispered, "Forgiveness. You need to learn how to forgive."

Sam waited for Balashi to say more. Instead, he only heard the chirping of crickets and the croaking of frogs mingled with his own intermittent crying. After a moment, Sam's sobs stopped. He looked up at Balashi and asked, "What do you mean, forgive? Who? Why? What are you talking about?"

Balashi answered slowly. "Forgive yourself. And your father."

Sam shook his head. "I've done too many bad things to be able to forgive myself," he said. "And I can never forgive my father. Because of him, both my mother and my brother are dead. Because of him I'll always walk with a limp. Because of him." Sam's voice choked off. He turned and reached out for Balashi, burying his head in the *asu's* multi-colored robe. Sam let his tears freely fall down his cheeks again.

Balashi hugged Sam tightly. "Son," he soothed, "forgiveness does not mean you excuse someone's behavior or pretend that nothing happened. It means you deal with the pain and go on. You choose not to seek revenge."

Balashi put his hands on Sam's shoulders, gently drew him back, and looked into his eyes. "What do we always take with us when we visit the sick?" he asked.

Sam wiped his cheeks with the back of his hands and sniffled. "Our pouches with our medicines and tools," he replied.

"And do we always have what we need?"

"Most of the time," Sam responded, and then sniffed again. "But not always."

Balashi pursed his lips. "Most of the time, parents carry a pouch that gives them the tools they need to take care of their children, to love them, provide for them, protect them. Your father didn't have any of those tools in his pouch."

Sam imagined his father carrying a pouch like the one Balashi carried when he visited the sick. In his mind, he opened his father's pouch. He saw nothing inside. Empty. Sam began to tremble. He looked up into the stars. "Maybe if I had been a better son." Hot tears spilled out onto his cheeks. "Maybe if I hadn't cried so much as a baby he wouldn't have thrown me across the room and I wouldn't have this limp. Maybe."

Balashi also looked up into the sky. "No, Sam," he interrupted. "As I said before, children shouldn't have to earn their parents' love. Love should already be in a parent's pouch. Parents must teach their children right and wrong; but providing for, loving, and protecting your children should be unconditional."

Sam felt like he had swallowed a ball of fire. He tried to push it out, but it wouldn't budge. Sam and Balashi quietly looked at the stars for a while. Sam finally broke the silence. "My mother's pouch wasn't empty, but she died while Yasmah and I were hired out to Ninkas. I thought my brother's pouch was empty because he never stood up for me when my father beat me. But then Yasmah died saving my life. My father's pouch," Sam hesitated. "My father's pouch is empty."

Chapter 14

The night of the commissioning banquet finally arrived. Sam's stomach felt like the juggling entertainers who performed somersaults on the sides and rear of the hall. What if his plan fell through? He wished Enlil were here with him, but Balashi had ordered Enlil to one more week of bed rest.

"Are you all right?" Amata asked as they walked through the banquet hall toward their assigned table.

Sam felt the shadow of a smile flit across his face and then disappear. Amata squeezed his hand before they sat down at their seats. Balashi sat down on the other side of Amata. She looked beautiful in her white tunic, blue shawl with gold trim, and blue slippers. Sam noticed that the lapis lazuli necklace also hung around her neck.

Sam glanced around the huge hall. In the front, facing the guests, sat Iridu, the former Susa captain, and his wife. On the other side of Iridu sat Lurs, dressed in his fine red soldier's tunic ribbed with silver stripes. Next to Lurs sat his wife, her black hair elegantly coiffed and secured with a sparkling gold clasp. Sam turned to look at the guests seated at the tables behind him. He spotted Ninkas at a table near the back of the room. Earlier in the week

Sam had discovered that Ninkas was staying at a local inn. Lurs had found a way to "accidentally" meet Ninkas and also invite him to the banquet. After dinner Lurs and Sam would put their plan into motion.

Sam had never seen such a feast: legume soup, chate melon, figs, grapes, pears, plums, pomegranates, cheese, and a sesame seed bread made from a fine flour such as Sam had never tasted. Then came the main dishes. They included pork, mutton, veal, duck, pigeon, and a variety of fish. Sam had just bitten into his after-dinner truffle when Lurs came over and tapped him on the shoulder.

"It's time," Lurs whispered in his ear.

Sam led Lurs toward the back of the hall where he had seen Ninkas sitting earlier that evening. In the crowd of people Sam had difficulty finding him again. "There," Sam said as he finally pointed him out. He saw Ninkas sitting next to a large man in a mustard-colored robe.

Lurs nodded and then cautioned Sam. "Stay back here where you won't be seen."

Sam stepped behind a large stone statue of a lion and nodded in agreement.

Lurs approached Ninkas and whispered something in his ear.

Ninkas smiled, got up from his table, and walked over to the back right corner of the room where he slipped behind a curtain.

"Now for the second part of our plan," Lurs whispered to Sam after Ninkas left.

Sam and Lurs scouted the room for a glimpse of Negrel.

"There, second table on the right," Sam told Lurs after he spotted the caravan driver.

Lurs smiled. "I told Negrel to meet me at the end of the meal in the back of the hall by the winged bull statue. He should be moving over there any moment."

Just as Lurs predicted, Negrel got up from his table and walked to the back of the room. The winged bull statute stood right in front of the curtain that hid the skulking form of Ninkas.

Lurs joined Negrel next to the winged bull statue. Sam hid once again behind the lion statue.

Negrel tugged on his beard asked Lurs, "So which jewel does her highness favor tonight?"

"An emerald," Lurs advised.

"Then an emerald gift it is," Negrel said and then smiled.

Suddenly, Ninkas came out from behind the curtain and put a knife to Negrel's back.

Lurs pretended not to notice and quietly walked away.

Sam remained hidden behind the stone lion.

"Don't say a word and don't turn around," Ninkas told Negrel in a hushed voice. "I hear you have my stolen jewels, and I want them back."

"What are you talking about?" Negrel asked as he tried to turn around. Ninkas only pressed the knife more firmly against him.

"You know what I'm talking about," Ninkas scratched out. "The jewels stolen from me by a crippled boy and then later stolen from him by you!"

"I, I only have one on me, the ruby," Negrel whined. "Here. Take it and leave me be." Negrel slowly withdrew the ruby from his waist pouch and slipped it to Ninkas.

A guard, noticing Negrel and Ninkas' discussion, began to walk towards them.

"What? No diamond or emerald?" Ninkas whispered quickly. "I'm not sure I believe you, but we'll finish this conversation later."

Just then, an official at the front stood and called for everyone's attention. "As you know, tonight we honor the outgoing captain of the Susa battalion and welcome him as the new commander of the Royal Battalions." Applause arose from the audience.

"Commander Iridu, would you like to say a few words?" the official asked.

Commander Iridu, dressed in full uniform, dagger at his side, rose to his feet. "I am honored to receive my new position and equally pleased to publicly announce my replacement in Susa, the recently promoted Captain Lurs."

Lurs, who had returned to his place next to his wife, now stood up and took a bow. Another round of applause arose from the audience.

The official at the head table motioned for the applause to die down and then announced, "Commander Iridu, there are a few of us here who would like to show you our gratitude for the years of service you gave as captain of the Susa Battalion. Would those people now come forward?"

A line of about twenty-five people formed, each person bearing some kind of gift. Commander Iridu and his wife received everyone individually, thanked each person, and then accepted the gift presented to them.

Negrel and Ninkas stood near the end of the line. Negrel tugged on his beard. Ninkas shifted his weight from one foot to the other. Finally, Negrel stood in front of Commander Iridu and his wife. He bowed low and handed the captain a leather pouch.

Commander Iridu, still seated behind the banquet table, withdrew an emerald from the pouch and held it up. "You are from Susa, are you not?" the commander asked Negrel.

Negrel cleared his throat. "Yes sir. I am a caravan driver from Susa. My name is Negrel. It would please me greatly if you and your wife would accept my gift."

Captain Iridu stood. "It shouldn't be difficult for me to accept your gift, Caravan Driver Negrel, since this emerald was mine to begin with!"

"What?" Negrel stepped back in surprise.

Captain Iridu withdrew the dagger from his side and placed the emerald into one of the indentations on the dagger's hilt. It fit perfectly. "Guards, seize this man!" the captain shouted.

As soldiers stepped forward to grab Negrel, Ninkas began to slink away.

Lurs now stood up and whispered something to Commander Iridu. The commander, with dagger still in hand, instructed his guards to seize Ninkas. Within seconds soldiers apprehended the landlord and placed him front of Commander Iridu.

"And whom do we have here?" the commander questioned Ninkas.

"I am a landlord and creditor from the Zagros Mountains who does business in Susa," Ninkas managed to scratch out.

"And you were in line to offer a token of gratitude?" Commander Iridu inquired.

"Ah, just this." Ninkas pulled out a bag from within his tunic and handed it to Commander Iridu.

The commander withdrew a ruby from the bag and held it up for all to see. "This is very interesting," Commander Iridu remarked. "Two men from Susa, each bearing a jewel that happens to fit exactly into an indentation on my bronze dagger!" Iridu fit the ruby in the top indentation on his dagger's hilt. "You were an innkeeper in Susa five years ago, were you not?" Commander Iridu asked Ninkas.

"Yes sir," Ninkas managed to say.

"An innkeeper who one night took advantage of a new captain who had too much to drink? You stole these jewels from my dagger the first night I spent in Susa!"

"No sir," Ninkas squeaked out. "These jewels were stolen from me by a crippled boy. His father is now in jail because he couldn't pay off the debts he owed me. I, I."

The commander returned his dagger to its sheath and folded his arms across his chest. "According to Hammurabi's Code," the commander quoted, "'if any one loses an article and finds it in the possession of another and it is proved to be stolen property, the thief shall be put to death'. I think if we search both you and the caravan driver, we will find the third missing stone, the diamond. Guards, search them, and then take them away. We will let the courts decide their fate!"

Chapter 15

After Negrel and Ninkas were led away, Amata stared at Sam wide-eyed and asked, "What just happened?"

Sam began to explain the trap he and Lurs had set for the two criminals, but was suddenly interrupted by the oohs and ahhs of the crowd. A large brown bear just emerged from a side hallway led by a bear trainer dressed in a silky golden-colored robe. The evening's entertainment had begun.

After the bear trainer came snake charmers. Sam sat in awe as he watched three snake charmers lure venomous cobras out of their baskets, hypnotizing them to rise up eight to ten feet in the air. The cobras' large-hooded heads swayed in rhythm with the charmers' double-piped flutes, causing Sam to also sway in his seat. Next, a group of musicians with lyres and harps came out to accompany a group of female dancers who clapped small cymbals or rattled tambourines as they performed.

During the dance Amata poked Sam. "So, what were you saying about you and Lurs?" she whispered.

Sam leaned closer and explained. "When your father and I first visited Commander Iridu to examine his broken arm, I noticed that he had three indentations on his dagger. It reminded me of the footsteps you left in the mud that day we went down to the river. The empty spaces in the dagger meant that something had been there that was now missing."

But what does that have to do with the two men who were just taken away?" Amata interrupted.

Sam smiled. "I'm getting to that," he said. "I also thought about the beautiful gown you bought, along with the shawl and the shoes – three beautiful things that went together. Then it clicked. The jewels were three beautiful stones that went together, but had been stolen from their original setting."

"The commander's dagger," Amata interrupted again.

Sam nodded. "I guessed that Ninkas must have stolen the jewels from the commander."

"And your brother stole them from Ninkas, and then the caravan driver stole them from you." Amata smiled wide.

Sam nodded again. "And, according to Hammurabi's Code, a person cannot be convicted of theft unless the stolen property is found in his possession. That's when Lurs and I decided to lure Ninkas and Negrel here, and to get each of them to present at least one of the jewels to the commander."

Sam hadn't noticed that the dancing had stopped until he heard the official's voice in the front of the hall call for everyone's attention.

"In addition to honoring Commander Iridu for his new commission as the Royal Battalion Commander and Captain Lurs as the new Susa Battalion Captain, we have one more commission to announce this evening."

Heads turned and a murmur arose from the crowd as people offered opinions as to what that new commission might be.

The official raised a hand to quiet the crowd. "The court advisers have taken notice of an extremely gifted *asu* here in Babylon, and have nominated him for a year of study in Egypt."

Sam and Amata looked at each other with open mouths.

"And this special award goes to Balashi ben Nahor," the official finished.

Applause immediately went up from the crowd. Commander Iridu rose to his feet. Sam then saw the judge and the priest that he and Balashi had treated also rise to their feet. About thirty more men stood, all applauding and smiling at Balashi. The official at the front motioned Balashi forward.

Balashi went to the front and bowed in front of Commander Iridu and the official. For the first time, Sam thought, Balashi almost looked speechless. The official handed Balashi a tablet and asked him to say a few words.

Balashi cleared his throat and then said, "Many thanks to those who have bestowed this honor upon me. Many thanks to our great King Hammurabi for giving me this opportunity to learn even more about the healing arts. I do not take this responsibility lightly. I will endeavor to learn all I can from the Egyptians and then return here to share that knowledge with all the great *asus* of Babylon."

The next morning as the early rays of sun warmed Sam's bedroom, he took time to ponder the events of the last few days. Before the banquet Balashi told Sam that he had visited his father by himself. Dagon had agreed to let Balashi adopt Sam in return for a sum that Balashi would not disclose to Sam. Balashi had also offered to help Sam find his uncle in Tyre if Sam still wanted to learn the bronzemaking trade. Now, thanks to Balashi's new commission in Egypt, Sam also had another option. If he didn't want to go to Tyre, he could accompany Balashi and Amata to Egypt where he'd learn even more about the healing arts. So many choices!

No one spoke at breakfast that morning. As Amata stirred her barley meal, she opened her mouth several times to speak but then closed it again. Finally, Sam broke the silence. "So, I hear the weather is very nice in Egypt this time of year!"